MR SHADOW

— AND THE —

NIGHT

— OF THE —

FOUR CRIMES

ANKIT ARYA

ISBN
Hardcase 979-8-89673-729-2
Paperback 979-8-89610-343-1

DEDICATION

This is for my family and friends who have stood by me and have always encouraged my artistic endeavours. This is also dedicated to 20-year-old me who thought up this idea but didn't have the tools or the know-how to bring it to life. I wish I could tell him that the story stuck with me all these years, and now the whole world can enjoy it.

CONTENTS

Acknowledgement...7

Author's Note & Foreword 9

Chapter 1   The Phone Call.......................... 13

Chapter 2   The Meeting 20

Chapter 3   The Date 30

Chapter 4   The Mistaken Identity............... 40

Chapter 5   The Job 46

Chapter 6   Back to the Future Present 54

Chapter 7   Dave's Excellent Adventure 59

Chapter 8   Riley's Wily Time....................... 66

Chapter 9   Bob's Job.................................... 72

Chapter 10   Thickening of the Plot............... 86

Chapter 11   What Do We Do Now? 99

Chapter 12   Why the Antagonism? 106

Chapter 13   It's Time 114

Chapter 14   Surprise 120

Chapter 15   French Food 130

Chapter 16   Almost There............................ 145

Chapter 17   Don't Ruin the Carpet.............. 151

Chapter 18   Something Doesn't Add Up 161

Chapter 19   It's the Number of That
             Pizza Place.................................. 167

Chapter 20   Honesty and a Proposal 177

Chapter 21   So What Will You
             Two Have? 193

Chapter 22   Cocktail Dress, Fishnet
             Stockings and High Heels......... 202

Chapter 23   Is Anybody Home?..................... 211

Chapter 24   Operation "Fly the Coop" 224

Chapter 25   The Whole Truth 237

Chapter 26   A Whole Truth Later.................. 246

Chapter 27   Money, War, and Peace.............. 254

Chapter 28   The End.................................... 263

ACKNOWLEDGEMENT

This book wouldn't have been possible without:

My family and friends who've supported my creative endeavours, especially writing, through all these many years and have encouraged me to share it with the world. I was always apprehensive, but I know now they were right.

The extraordinary Akanksha Jain who designed the eye-catching cover. The talented team at Notion Press, especially Shwetha, Jewel, Rani and Rashmi, for working with me on this book, which I hold dear to my heart. They helped me shape this manuscript into the book we're all proud of today. For their continued efforts to market it and reach the largest audience possible.

Author's Note & Foreword

This is a story that's been festering (in a good way) in my mind for almost a decade and a half. The inception of it came when I was 20. I wanted to write a screenplay for a crime thriller set in London inspired by Guy Ritchie and Matthew Vaughn films. Moreover, I wanted to add pulp and neo-noir elements to it. I had the perfect setup, everything else I didn't. I was 20. I wrote a screenplay of it back then and was very proud of it. It was mostly terrible. But the central idea was something that stuck with me.

When I was 28, I thought about turning it into a book. I had just finished work on a film that took 2 years to make but had aged me 5 years. I needed a break. A change. I began writing it down. Managed a few chapters but abandoned it like most writing projects. There was other work to do that was more pressing.

Then came the pandemic. Months with nothing to do but stay at home. I managed to find the time needed to get a lot of writing done. I finished this script of a series I had been writing on and off for months. Once that was done, I happened to chance upon those initial chapters I had written. They needed some work but it was a good foundation. I spent the next few months writing a vast portion of the book, finishing 2/3rds of it. And then COVID restrictions were removed. We could work again. And as destiny would have it, the book went into the back burner. Away from my thoughts as there was much else to be done. Like earning a living.

Then came the tail end of monsoon 2024. A film I'd been working on was delayed for a few months. Ad shoot work was there but had slowed down. Nothing but time on my hands. I began compiling my first poetry book but that barely took any time. I kept wondering what I could do. How do I make the most of this time? And the thought came like a spark. A weak ember that soon became a pyre too large to ignore. Something inside me that beckoned me to get this done. To see it through. To make my 20-year-old self happy. And I did. Spent 2 months on end, reading, writing and revising it every day till my family asked me to take a break. It consumed me. And I loved every bit of it. It's now finally done. Or so I thought. The editing process of the book gave me anxiety and all I could see were places in the book to make improvements. So, I did just that. Made improvements and tweaks over the next few months wherever I could. And now it's finally done. The whole process has been nerve-wrecking but exciting. And I know looking back, I will say the same thing. It consumed me. And I loved every bit of it. I've said this twice now in the same paragraph, so you know it's true.

If you were to ask me why I think you should read it? Well, the answer is simple. I think it's a story that's interesting, entertaining, thrilling, funny, sad, and outrageous. It deserves to be told. It deserves to be shared with the world. It deserves to be made into a film (production houses call me). At least I think so. But I know it's true. Otherwise, it wouldn't have festered and grown in my mind for a decade and a half. And I hope readers of this love it as much as I loved writing it.

—— CHAPTER 1 ——

THE PHONE CALL

A single bare lightbulb dangled from the ceiling. Its filament flickered from time to time. What it really needed was a china-ball cover to spread its glow, but for now, it did the job. The yellowish tungsten light reminded Darren of an angel's halo. Maybe that's what enamoured him so much. It was real yet so surreal. A page out of a fairytale book that had come to life. He always imagined seeing a halo would bring him good fortune. He couldn't argue with that logic right now. Darren believed in God as a kid. Then he grew up and stopped having imaginary friends. But this bulb in its finite foreverness made him think things over one more time. He could describe the bulb and its flickering to anyone in the world, and they would understand. The bulb united classes, countries, races, and religions. It was the only real thing he could think of at this moment.

The bulb spread its light onto a table. A rusty old thing that needed more than just a polish. It needed to be thrown away or used as firewood so it could have one last use in this world. The table was real too, but for Darren today reality was a bit of it's axis. *"That's a lot of money"* he thought to himself. So many pieces of paper with the face of Her Majesty and that same stern look. He had always hated the queen though he had never met her or even seen her at a distance. He kinda liked her face now. Maybe he had just warmed up to it.

Five million quid all in all. Not bad for a four-man small-time gang with most of its members in their late twenties. In fact, it was good. More than good. It was fucking great. It wasn't long ago they were stealing purses off frightened old ladies to have a slice of bread. That too the rotten kind. Not the good stuff with all the sesame seeds and other things the middle classes crave for on their bread.

But now it was different. It was going to stay different. Darren tried to recollect it all. Where did all this start? The bulb and its halo, the surreal table with the 5 million in cash between the four of them. And then he remembered. The thought came rushing back. One of those lightbulb moments from those old-timey cartoons.

It had begun with a phone call.

A week ago during an ungodly hour, Darren was snug asleep in his little whittle room. It was a small shabby studio council flat somewhere near Hackney Central Station. The oh-so original room had a pathetic excuse for a queen-sized bed in its centre. At a 45-degree angle from its lower right side was a small television conveniently placed at a suitable viewing angle. The walls were grimy, and the weird green paint that covered them was at least a decade old. In all fairness, it was a hellhole. But it was a hellhole with a decently sized, surprisingly clean, and modern washroom which made you forget that the closet didn't have a rod for hanging anything. And the curtains were terrible.

Darren, in his snug as a bug in a rug sleep, was dreaming of fireflies and endless days of gorgeous London summers. He was lying on a blanket in the middle of Hyde Park, breathing in the pollen and freshness of other summer things that more educated people know about. The butterflies took flight. Next to him was the only person who ever made him happy. As he looked into her eyes, saying nothing, he knew he wanted to stay in this dream forever.

The phone rang. It rang loud and it rang true. At first, it felt like a part of the dream during which his butler Jeeves with a gold-framed monocle and a posh accent brought him his telephone on a silver tray with piles of cocaine and an unfinished Mars bar. But sleep gave way to a soulless waking. It was mid-October 2007. London had long let go of long sunny days. It was raining outside with a terribly chilly breeze. The phone still rang. Darren drags his lifeless half in REM sleep body to the other side of the bed where the phone was.

"Hello." said Darren in a weak-willed voice and coughed half his lungs out. He had smoked way too much that day.

"Hello, Darren." said the voice at the other end of the phone. It was a man's voice. Smooth, bourbon-drinking, cigar-smoking voice that had a subtle softness to it. For unimaginative readers, imagine the voice of Humphrey Bogart.

"Who is this and how do you know my name?" Darren, who was now wide awake. The other man's voice and resolve gave Darren enough reason not to fall back asleep again.

"Well, I know a lot of things about you. Consider me your friend."

"What kind of friend calls in the middle of the fucking night?"

"The kind of friend who is excited to make a proposition."

"Oh yeah! What kind of proposition?"

"Not here. Not on the phone. It's too impersonal. Face to face."

"Whatever you want to tell me, you can say it on the phone. If you can't, then I guess this is goodbye." Darren had found the sleep he had been deprived of. The phone call seemed like a cruel joke from someone close. He had just about had enough of such immature shenanigans and was about to put the phone down when the voice on the other end shouted out two simple words.

"Two million."

Darren did not mishear it. He wished he had, but he wished he hadn't. He had one of his wishes come true.

"What's this job about?" asked Darren eagerly again.

"Like I said, not here. Face to face."

"When do you want to meet?"

"Sometime next year. How about Valentine's Day?"

Maybe it was the sudden loss of sleep, but Darren slowly made a move towards a notepad and pen to note down the date.

"NOW, YOU DUMB FUCK!" said the voice on the other end.

Darren was no longer sleepy. "Where should I meet you?"

"Close to Hackney Market. The alley by the little pizza place that sells little doughnut-shaped slices."

"Flaming Nero's?" Darren asked inquisitively.

"Yes, that's the one. You should know all about it." And the man at the other end laughed, what could only be described as a comic book super villain laugh. But it wasn't a wholehearted laugh but rather a quiet snicker.

Darren knew that this man knew way too much. It was either that big a job or that elaborate a joke. "Alright. I'll be there in about twenty. But who's calling? I still don't know your name."

"And you don't need to. But you can call me Mr Shadow."

"Shadow?"

"No, Mr Shadow. Twenty minutes." said the man who wished to be called Mr Shadow in a "whiny tone that should rightfully belong to a sixteen-year-old white girl from the American suburbs who wanted a unicorn for her birthday but got only a pony" before he cut the call.

Darren pinched himself hard just to make sure he wasn't still dreaming. He turned on the light. It was a solitary bulb dangling from the ceiling. What was missing was a china-ball.

—— CHAPTER 2 ——

THE MEETING

The lamp post had a wider glow; a more pronounced halo. And Darren stood in the middle of its warmth. This, however, was not enough. The weather was unforgiving. The days were all windy with patchy, splashy rains. Darren stood wearing a woolly jumper, but it made no difference. The only respite here was the halo. The lamp post and its angelic-ness. Beyond it was the darkness of East London late at night. Right up till the next lamp post, which was fifteen feet away. Even so, Darren felt like he stood on an island. The island of the halo. Surrounded by darkness all around. He stared at the light and wished it would never go out. He was the happiest moth in the liveliest of flames. But he had been waiting for almost an hour now, and there was still no sign of Mr Shadow. *What a silly name*, he thought to himself. Not the kind of name a grown man should have.

He looked around once again with squinted eyes to see if anything else was in sight. Nothing! Not a soul on the road. Not even a neon sign left on accidentally. The city that never slept had tucked itself in and called it a day. Darren wanted to call it a day as well. It was getting late. Sleep kept finding ways back to him. To make matters worse, the only thoughts that entered Darren's mind were ones he would have preferred to have kept out. *Was this meeting a joke? If so, who had planned it? Or worse, was it the coppers?" Had they set him up in some fiendish form of entrapment?* Two million as bait was way too cruel. That amount of money would have made a straight man meander his ways, and Darren. Well, Darren was as bent as they came.

"Going to prison again won't be so bad." Darren mumbled to himself, almost reassuringly. Darren was tall and lithe but strong. He could take care of himself in prison. In fact, he had the first time around when he went in for breaking and entering. Darren deserved to go to prison again as far as he was concerned. He hadn't forgiven himself for what he had done 2 years ago. And he had never told her. Her! He had almost forgotten about her in his greed. The only person who really truly matters.

It was a year and a half ago, and it took place a stone's throw away at a little pizza place that had a gimmick and a half. It sold doughnut-shaped slices and called itself Flaming Nero's. It was a highly popular place among the gay community, arsonists, and eight-year-old white middle-class girls. The place was smallish, had tacky purple plastic seating, and god-awful fluorescent lighting that reflected like a disco ball on the white-tiled floor. This made the barely edible food look even more bleak. To make things even more perfect, the cafe had a funny smell, which was disinfectant with a hint of lemon and tangerine for an extra-long-lasting clean feel™.

Darren stood behind the counter wearing an apron that could rob a man's dignity and a hat that spat on it. But after prison, this was the only place that hired him. The only place that took him in. And it barely covered the bills. Prison was supposed to reform him. Not confine him. But all that was for another day. This day, however, seemed just like any other for Darren. Nothing special except maybe spring was finally giving up. Summer was coming! And then she walked in.

French beret-wearing, cheap Chinese-made imitation Italian suit-wearing all-American girl. She walked slowly to the counter where Darren waited. He measured each of her steps and remembered the clitter-clatter her shoes made as she walked slowly towards him. She was a fair, attractive girl with a small nose, large brown eyes, and very sharp features. She had long flowing black hair which she stroked back with her right hand, giving it a slight flick. She glanced at Darren and smiled. That smile! Oh, that smile!

"Hello," she said in the most seductive of voices.

"Hi," said Darren, clearly smitten.

"How long have you been waiting out in the cold?"

"Excuse me," asked Darren, confounded and confused.

"How long have you been waiting out in the cold?" came the question again. Only this time, the voice sounded a lot like Humphrey Bogart.

Darren snaps out of his dream and turns around. He sees a large shadow of a man painted on the alley wall. He squints his eyes to find the man. The man was tall and lean like him. He wore black boots, black pants, a black trench coat, and a hat.

"Quit daydreaming. It's the middle of the night," said the Humphrey Bogart voice.

"Mr Shadow?" asked Darren dumbly.

"In the flesh," said Mr Shadow dramatically. "Now, come. Follow me." And he was off.

Darren waited for a second before he began to follow Mr Shadow. He wanted to catch up, but Mr Shadow was soft and nimble on his feet. He took a left turn into the alley and then a sharp right, another right, and then a left before entering an alley that had a little door to a small hallway leading into a room on one side. Darren saw the door was open and a light flickered on. He cautiously entered the hallway and then the room only to find a table in the centre of it, with Mr Shadow sitting on the other side facing him. There was a strong light behind Mr Shadow. He couldn't see his face. In fact, he hadn't seen his face until now. He could only see a silhouette.

"Sit!" said the voice with a certain sternness that made Darren yield.

Darren was normally an unsettled sitter. Never being able to sit still. But in that moment, he sat noiselessly. "If only he could peek at his face," the thought came rushing, but Darren thought it was against better judgement to try something stupid. At least for now.

After a long pause, Mr Shadow spoke. "Do you want a cigarette?"

"No," said Darren instantly. He had wanted a cigarette.

"Do you mind if I smoke?"

Darren shook his head. Mr Shadow took out a fancy-looking cigar and set it alight. He smoked it for a few moments, enjoying its flavour.

"Nothing like a good cigar."

Mr Shadow smoked as if he had all the time in the world. Darren looked as though he had almost run out of it.

"Would you like a drink?" inquired Mr Shadow.

"No! I wouldn't like a drink," retorted Darren in a more snappy tone.

"You sound like you need one."

"WHAT I NEED," snapped Darren, lightly tapping the table before calming his cranky self down, "is to know why I'm here?"

Mr Shadow takes another few puffs of his cigar. "As I mentioned, I have a job for you. It's highly dangerous. But the reward is worth it."

"Two million you mentioned."

"Yes. That's how much."

Darren thought about it deeply. He thought about what he could do with that money. A new home, a new TV, and a brand-new diamond ring for… But before he could finish that thought, he began having certain other thoughts again. The ones he'd have preferred to keep out. The problem with Darren was that while he thought deeply about the proposition, he didn't think about it for too long.

"I'll take it," he sounded desperate saying it.

"Wow! You're more stupid than I thought. I haven't even told you what you're doing."

"I'm not stupid. Just motivated. What do I have to do?" replied Darren with pride.

"Next Friday, you break into this address," Mr Shadow puts a small piece of paper on the desk with an address typed out on it.

"How big is this place?"

"It's an office space. Two rooms. A large waiting room and a smaller cabin. In the cabin, there is a safe. I need you to break it open. Shouldn't be too hard for a man of your skill."

"I don't think so," said Darren. "I've been breaking into my mum's liquor cabinet since I could walk."

"Well, yes, that's very nice," said Mr Shadow, dismissing Darren's ramblings about his childhood. "Inside the safe, you shall find 2 million pounds' worth of gold, cash, and jewellery. All unmarked and there for the taking. And you shall find a key."

"What key?"

"Human nature is funny. I mention 2 million pounds in cash and all you're interested in is a key."

"What's so special about this key?"

"Nothing you need to know about. You keep the cash and you take the key and…" Mr Shadow moved forward, stubbed his cigar messily out on a skull-faced ashtray, turned his body around ever so slightly, grabbed hold of a heavy-looking manila envelope, put it softly on the table, took out another bit of paper from it with a typed-out address and put it on the table. "… deliver it to this address. Just slide it under the door." All the while making sure that his face never touched the light.

Darren moves his hand towards the paper, and before he could pick it up, Mr Shadow grabs hold of his hand.

"No later than 2 am."

Mr Shadow lets go of his hand. He pushes the envelope towards him.

"All the details are in here."

Darren puts his hand inside the envelope, but it wasn't the details on paper that bothered him. They were well-laid-out instructions, do's and don'ts, a map route to take around the city, etc. The pinpoint micromanagement of it all was a thing of beauty. This had to go perfectly. What bothered Darren was the gun. Darren picked it up, saw it was loaded, had a silencer attached, and the safety was on.

"Why the gun?" asked Darren cautiously. He hadn't used a gun. Not since that night.

"Inside the file are details of who you're stealing from."

"Yes, but why the gun?" interrupted Darren.

"Like I was saying. Inside the file are details of who you're stealing from. I'm sure you will find keeping a warm gun ready as the appropriate course of action."

Darren wanted to mount a reply. But what he did was just quietly nod. Two million. The answer to a lot of questions Darren had in his mind. Darren packed the file up and put the gun in his coat pocket. He rose and began to make his way to the door.

"Oh, and one more thing," said Mr Shadow in a booming voice. "You so much as mention my name to anyone, and I will kill you in the most unimaginable way imaginable."

"Why the antagonism? It makes me sad. We're on the same team, aren't we?" retorted Darren with a smile on his face. Having a gun with him made him feel a little more foolhardy.

Mr Shadow sniggered a bit. "I like you. But don't fuck this up. And if I find you telling any of those jerk-offs about this job…"

"You'll kill me in the most unimaginable way imaginable. Yeah, I know."

"No, no," laughed Mr Shadow a little louder this time. "I'll kill them instead. You have a job to do. Once that's done, then you have my permission to die."

Darren pinched himself again just to make sure he wasn't still dreaming. He wasn't.

—X—

—— CHAPTER 3 ——

THE DATE

It was Friday. It had been a regular day at work for Darren. Eight hours in fluorescent hell. But now the time had come. This is what he had been waiting for. This is what he had been dreading. He entered his home with a heavy heart. He had a few hours of contemplation ahead of him. And then the biggest test of his life.

He had the manila envelope placed on his bed. He had memorised the details. The addresses. The route. The "Everything". This had to go perfectly. This was going to be perfect. All week long he hadn't opened his mouth about it to anyone. Especially not to his mates. He had promised Mr Shadow. Mr Shadow had made him paranoid. Every night, Darren studied the details for hours on end. He picked up the gun to check it. It was a beauty. Top of its line. A 9mm with a full clip. All 9 bullets. But he only had one clip. Darren thought about the last time he used a gun. It had been over 2 years. That was a long time to live with guilt. It had eaten away a large part of his soul. He felt a heaviness in his heart.

A sinking feeling that something wrong is going to happen. And in those thoughts, he knew deep down inside that he shouldn't go through with this job.

He was interrupted by a phone call.

It was his cellphone. Darren reached into his pocket to find the little measly thing. It slipped out of his hand and fell to the floor. He picked up his trusted little burner and stopped vacant. It was her. She was calling. Darren lingered for a moment before answering. He did not know what to say to her. He didn't want to lie to her. He decided to wing it and answered the call. Not answering was worse.

"Hey," Darren knew he was best at something when he was under pressure. Maybe he should go through with the job, he thought to himself briefly.

"Hello, you," answered the woman from the other end in a sweet, serene voice. "Where are you?"

"I just reached home," Darren did not know what to tell her. It was Friday night. In *couplespeak*, it was date night. But Darren had a date with destiny instead. He had never told her about his prison term. He had tried to keep that world away from her and had been quite successful until now. But now his worlds were colliding. "I think I'm going to sleep off. I don't feel so good." Yes! That could work. It was only half a lie. He did feel quite sick. But for different reasons.

"Are you okay, love? Do you want me to come over?" she asked in concern. "We could have a nice movie night in. It's your turn to pick."

It was Darren's turn to pick. Last movie night he was forced to watch 'The Notebook'. Not because she was into rom coms. But because it was set in her home state of South Carolina.

She continues. "We can watch Robot Cop. You've been going on and on about it forever. I can also pick up some shepherd's pie on the way."

"You mean 'Robocop'?" Darren smiles. She always wanted the best for him as he did for her.

"Robocop. Robot Cop. Same thing. So, what do you say? Want me to come over and heal you with some TLC?"

Darren was tempted to say yes and tell Mr Shadow to sod off. Especially since he had the bootleg of the extended version which he bought some weeks ago in Brick Lane. But he knew what had to be done. There was no turning back this late in the game. Mr Shadow had made that very clear. "No. That's quite all right, love. I'll see you tomorrow. I just need some sleep. I love you."

"I love you too. Take care."

And Darren hung up the phone. He handled that quite well. But he broke into tears the second he hung up. He did not like lying to her. But his whole relationship had been a lie. But it did not begin like this.

It started a year and a half ago in a small pizza place which sold a gimmick more than pizzas. She had just walked in with her long, gorgeous black hair, big brown eyes, small nose, and sharp features. Darren, in his tall, pale frame, stood waiting behind the counter and eyed her every step towards him.

"Hello," she said in the most seductive of voices.

"Hi," replied Darren, clearly smitten.

"I'd like to place an order, please," she continued.

In that moment, Darren lost all motor function in his body. This was quite common for men to experience when they're aroused by a woman. But Darren was exceptionally good at this, and he looked especially special when this happened to him. Plus, the spliff he shared with his colleague Vladamir during their tea break clearly didn't help.

"Excuse me. I'd like to order, please," she spoke out again.

Darren snapped out and began to answer in a half-confused, rapid manner. "Yes, of… of course! What would you like?"

"Ummm! I guess I'm not sure. Maybe you could suggest something. Something light and fresh."

"Uh. This is a greasy spoon. I'm sorry, but you're not going to have much of a choice here."

"Well, it's just that I'm new here. And I don't understand half of the things you Brits write."

"Well, what kind of food do you want?"

"I told you. Something light and fresh."

"I think the best thing we have here is the fat-free calzone."

"Is it really fat-free?"

Darren leaned in closer to her and whispered to her softly, "No, not really. But if we told the truth, it won't sell as well, and it sells really, really well."

"Whatever. I'll have one with chicken."

"That'll be 3.75."

"Do you take credit cards?"

"No, sorry. Cash only."

"Dammit. I don't have any cash with me."

"There's a cashpoint right around the corner," Darren pointed out.

"You mean an ATM?"

Americans! thought Darren. They speak American. Not English. The English speak English. And so does most of the world. Sort of. "Yes," replied Darren and smiled a dumb smile.

She smiled at Darren, slowly turned around and walked away. Darren whacked himself on his head. "You stupid wanker."

Darren had always been shy with women. He always left something unsaid. He also hesitated in taking that extra step. But something happened to him that day. He had never wanted someone so badly. He never felt a pang of desire as sharp as this one. *You'd be a fool not to follow her*, he thought to himself. Darren thought deeply about following her. Luckily, he didn't think too long about it either and took his apron off in a flash, shouted to his boss, Nick, that he was off for lunch and dashed out of the restaurant.

The girl had made her way to the cashpoint and stood in the short queue that had been formed. Darren walked quietly right behind her. He could smell her perfume. It smelled classy and inexpensive at the same time. This girl was as much a contradiction as him. She seemed like she also had 2 worlds she wanted to keep apart. The folks ahead of her, a middle-aged couple, had made their withdrawal and left the machine vacant for her use.

Darren had made the decision to follow her, but this was as futile as nipples on the batsuit unless he did something about it. It was time to take that plunge. But what should he say to her? What could he say? What could make him sound eloquent? Or at least not a wanker. While Darren thought this through, he realised she was taking longer than most people to withdraw cash.

"Could you hurry up, sweetheart? I'm in a bit of a rush," the words came tumbling out of Darren's mouth. He had a tendency to speak his mind. His mind, however, was full of thoughts that needed to be filtered. So it wasn't the best quality to have.

"Cool your jets. I'm almost done."

She collected her money and her card, tucked them into her little money satchel, which she kept inside her giant cream tote bag that went well with her well-fitted jacket and skirt. She turned around and saw it was Darren. "Oh, it's you. You look quite different without that apron. A lot less…" she didn't know what to say. "… Shit?"

The girl had a tongue on her. She was turning out to be a saucy one. Darren was slowly but surely falling in love with her. A rare occurrence for him that happened about once or twice a week. He knew he had to play it cool with her. "Why, thank you. Now if you don't mind, I only get thirty minutes for lunch," Darren inserted his card into the cashpoint and began to withdraw cash.

"Why don't you eat food at the place you work?" inquired the girl. She was about to leave but lingered just a second longer.

"Because it's disgusting," answered Darren with a wry smile. He figured she was still here. There had to be something she felt too.

"And you were about to let me eat it. How dare you?" The girl lightly hit Darren on his arm.

"OW!" screamed Darren, and out came his cash. He pocketed it and smiled at the girl.

"What kind of employee would I be if I shooed away potential customers?" He was happy with what he said and began to strut his way down the street. She stood there and watched Darren go before she ran up to him.

"Then where do you eat?"

"This little place 3 streets down."

"How's the food there?"

"Quite bland and tasteless. Still better than Flaming Nero's."

"What would your boss say if he heard you say all these things?"

She was a wily one. "Nothing. He'd just let me go."

"Well, I guess you're at my mercy then."

"Well, I guess I am. What do you want from me?" Oh, please let it be everything.

"A favour."

"Whatever you need."

"Show me this restaurant you speak of. I'm starving."

"I'm heading over there right now. Would you like to join me?"

"I'd love to."

"I'm Darren by the way."

And it was as simple as that. That's how it began for Darren and...

"Hi, Darren. Nice to meet you. I'm Judy," Darren and Judy.

— CHAPTER 4 —

The Mistaken Identity

Darren sat down by the door to cry a little. Crying always helped him. It got rid of things. Skeletons he'd been meaning to clean up. He rose and made his way to the cupboard. If he was going to do this thing, he needed to get ready. But then he stopped midway. Did he want to go through with it? He thought about it deeply one last time. And the answer his heart gave him was simple. "Do it." Two million was worth it. The times he did a job well were when he was either under pressure or didn't think twice about it. Darren rushed to his cupboard and took out a pair of black trousers, a black t-shirt, a black trench coat, black leather gloves, a hat, and a woolly cap that had eye and nose holes cut out. He reached under his bed and took out a pair of heavy black boots to wear instead of his knock-off Nike trainers. He laid all his clothes out neatly on the bed.

He made his way to the small window and sat on the folding chair next to it. He made himself a quick rollie and lit it. As he smoked, he saw the traffic pass him by. It was a busy intersection he lived close to, and rush hour had only just ebbed away. Every bit of distraction helped him at the moment. He disrobed, grabbed a towel, and went to take a shower. The water was nice and warm, and with it, he cleansed his body. It felt like holy water was raining over him.

"The gun," that was the only thought in his head, though. The distractions hadn't worked. He peeked from behind the curtain through the open door and saw the gun lying on the bed, pointing right at him. Darren was good with a gun. Maybe too good. But he didn't like them because he knew what they could do.

It happened 2 years ago on a night quite the same. Darren was in the shower. A mysterious stranger slowly opened Darren's flat door with a pointed gun leading his way. He scanned the room cautiously before he noticed the sound of the shower. He turned around and made his way to the bathroom where Darren showered in serenity and peace. The mysterious man was of average height and bulky. An olive-toned chap with a 5 o'clock stubble and hair that looked like it was cut by a knife. He glided his way across the floor quieter than a tiger on a hunt. He was on a hunt as well. And he hadn't made a mistake. The prey was unaware.

Call it intuition or luck, but Darren turned around in the nick of time to see the shadow of the man through the shower curtain. On instinct, he leapt at him. The hunter had become the hunted. The mysterious stocky man got knocked off his feet, and the gun slipped from his hand away from both of them. Darren wore his bathrobe in a rush and went across his room to a crowbar that he had kept out, probably for a situation like this. The moment he grabbed it and turned around, the mysterious assailant was on him. He shoulder-tackled Darren up against the wall, not once, not twice, but thrice. The force of it made Darren drop the crowbar. The assailant grabbed hold of it instead. He put one hand on Darren's mouth and hit him on the gut. Darren winced in pain. He held onto the assailant's leg, crying.

"Please stop. Please."

The mysterious man dropped the crowbar at that moment. *"He listened to me,"* thought Darren. Darren thought wrong. The assailant takes out a Bowie knife from under his jacket. He knelt down and put it under Darren's throat. "Where is the money?"

"What money?" asked Darren, drowned in pain.

The assailant pressed the knife against his throat, making him bleed a bit. "Wrong answer."

Darren truly had no idea what the man was talking about, but he needed a distraction. "It's in the pillow covers."

The distraction worked. The man kicked Darren away and made his way to the pillowcase. Darren grabbed hold of his leg by his pants and pulled him so hard that he fell on his face to the floor. The knife never left the assailant's hand. Darren rose to his feet after what seemed like an eternity, grabbed hold of the crowbar and whacked the mysterious assailant right behind his kneecap.

Darren then made his way to his bathroom. "*That's where it fell,*" he remembered. "The gun," the only thought that was in his head. The mysterious assailant had limped his way to the pillow covers, but they were empty. Darren grabbed hold of the gun and slipped it into his bathrobe pocket, then leapt on the man and pinned him down on the bed.

"Who sent you?" asked Darren aggressively, choking him slightly.

The assailant had slipped the knife quietly into his pocket. He slid it out and slashed Darren across the stomach. Blood splattered all around. Darren grabbed his gut. The gash was deep, but not too deep.

The assailant charged at Darren with the knife, but Darren ducked and let him pass through. Darren picked up a pillow and threw it at the man. The man grabbed the pillow, but Darren shoulder-tackled him down. Pushed the pillow on his face. The assailant began to struggle and gasp for air. He grabbed hold of his knife and stabbed Darren through his left thigh. The gash had stunned him. This nearly destroyed him. Darren screamed in agony, which turned to anger. He reached for the gun, pointed it at the assailant's face. He didn't think about it deeply. He knew what he had to do. He pulled the trigger. The man who had struggled to the very edge of his existence ceased to exist at that very moment.

Darren snapped back to reality and noticed that he had been showering for way too long. He reached for his towel, wiped himself off, and decided to have another cigarette. As he smoked, he recalled the really crazy part of the story. The stocky assailant had come for his neighbour, who owed some serious drug money. Darren was both horrified and amused by this. He had killed a man in self-defence who did not really want to kill him. **"A story of mistaken identity always turns out badly. Mostly for the person who's wrongly identified."** Darren had always felt guilty for not coming clean. The body was never found. He had dumped it in the Thames. He had gotten away with murder. Then why didn't it feel good? What was wrong?

CHAPTER 5

THE JOB

It was a cold night with a brisk wind and a slightly annoying drizzle. "Typical London weather" thought Darren spitefully. It wasn't the wind or the chill that got to him, though; it was the droplets of water that kept making their way into his eyes. He was forced to keep his duffel bag down and take his gloves off over and over again to wipe his face.

The only people he found in the streets at that hour were pub-goers and young'uns prowling in the night. The perfect kind of bystanders, he thought and smiled. He quickened his pace. He didn't want to be late. He wanted to reach his destination by midnight.

The job at hand was simple. Break in and enter the office space. Locate the safe and crack it open. Any cash and valuables found inside would be his. Inside the safe would also be a golden key. Deliver the key to the required address. NO LATER THAN 2 AM. He remembered all the details. He had studied them end to end. This was a job that was going to require finesse. It was a job that required Darren. He wasn't going to fuck this up. He couldn't fuck this up, to be more specific.

There it was, a block away. He stopped walking and checked his watch. It was 11:58. He was on time. The office was a brick-armoured fortress on a corner plot with not a sign on it to be found. The only advantage that the peculiar structure gave Darren was that it was a ground floor. He could make a quick getaway if things went wrong. Just before the office was a dark, narrow running alley into which Darren quietly tucked himself. There were no CCTV cameras there, he noticed. Darren slipped on his mask and adjusted his leather gloves. It was go time.

Darren crept like a cat and approached the office building with caution. The main door was heavy, with a standard circular knob and a fancy key slot that used those new electronic coded keys. This was going to be time-consuming. Thirty minutes worth of work at least. That was no good. He was going to be late. In a moment of utter panic, Darren tried his hand at lady luck. He turned the knob around and gave the door a slight push. The door swung open.

Confounded and confused, Darren entered slowly, pointing his gun forward. Barely any streetlight crept into the fortress. Darren pulled the door shut behind him. He was now enveloped in near-complete darkness. All he could see was a sofa close to a window and a plant that sat in the corner. The light switch was just above it. He flicked it on. And jumped. And pointed his gun straight ahead.

A man sat on a table right next to another door. The door to the office! The man sat motionless. "What a clusterfuck this was turning out to be," thought Darren as he made his way across the room to the man. "No pulse," said Darren, holding the man's wrist. Exactly what he thought. The dead man had been shot in the chest. The bullet went straight in and stayed in there. The man's black coat made it hard to see the blood, which oddly enough didn't splatter much. This was the work of a professional.

Darren made his way to the office door. He turned the knob, and the door swung open. It, too, was unlocked. He wondered if he would have the same luck with the safe. The office was a cliché of a cliché. A plant in each corner, a large table in the middle. Three guest chairs and the biggest, most comfortable chair for the man who sat behind the table. This was the chair of a man of power. The one thing Darren liked about the office was that it had bare walls. No pretentious corporate works of art. It also meant that the safe was somewhere else, most probably under the table. Darren's assumption was right. "Occam's razor. The simplest explanation is probably the correct one." He heard the phrase in an American Medical Drama and began to use the phrase wherever he thought it fit.

The safe was a tricky one. It was old and sturdy. A really heavy piece of equipment. Breaking into this needed precision, time, and strength. He put his duffel bag down, unzipped it, and took out his tools and a stethoscope. Forty minutes of toiling later, the lock came undone. Darren rolled the lever, and the safe door opened slightly ajar. He pulled it open, and there it was. All the cash and gold Darren could ever imagine. It was right there. It was real, yet so surreal. Darren wanted to savour this moment, but he needed to get across town. And fast. Time was always against him. He began to pile his treasure into the duffel bag and closed the zip. He then began to examine the empty safe. "The Golden Key." He still hadn't found it. He thought about running away with the money. But what kind of person would that make him, he thought to himself. A dishonourable one came the answer. He wasn't that. He was just a thief.

He began prodding inside the safe before he noticed a secret compartment tucked away in one of its corners. He pressed a small hidden button and inside opened a secret compartment. He slipped his fingers inside the compartment and laid his hands on a long, cold metallic object. It was the key. He slowly took it out and held it up. It was a beautifully crafted key. It was an old-fashioned one with the bow designed like a rosebud. For a moment, Darren wanted the golden key more than the money. But it was only the briefest of moments.

Darren hurried his way out but he left the place as he found it. Without the 2 million, of course. He made his way through the dark alley and emerged from the other end a few moments later wearing a different set of clothes and a hat. He noticed a black cab down a block and began to run after it. The driver noticed him just before driving off.

The drop-off point for the key was a distance away, but Darren knew it wouldn't take so long.

Not at this hour. It was almost 1am. The city was beautiful at this time of the night. The streetlights and their halos, the pub-goers and the homeless, the markets and the roads. They were all the same, yet everything seemed different. Darren pinched himself to see if he wasn't dreaming. He wasn't. He pinched himself again, only this time he really dug his nails into it. He winced in pain. But he wasn't dreaming. He wasn't dreaming.

The black cab pulled over at an upper-middle-class block of flats in West Kensington that had seen better days. The seven-storey building did not have much security to speak of. A numbered code lock that required a five-digit passcode and no cameras. The passcode was in the details. Darren quickly keyed in the code and entered as if he owned the place. With the money he had in the duffel bag, he could buy a chunk of it, he thought. Or a large stretch of land somewhere out in the countryside. He hadn't completely decided what he was going to do with the money. A flat screen TV was number one on the list.

He walked down the beige-coloured hallway and into the lift. The flat was on the fifth floor. He got off the elevator and walked towards the flat. He checked his clock. It was 1:47. He was thirteen minutes early. This was perfect. He walked up to the flat door. The flat right opposite it had blaring music playing through the doors. Darren could barely hear his thoughts above the din. He slid the key under the door and quietly but swiftly paced away. The elevator hadn't left the floor, luckily. He entered the lift and pressed the button. He did not want to know who was at the other end of the door. The elevator door closed ever so slowly as Darren watched the flat door open and a man peeked out towards the elevator.

He ran out of the lift and out of the building and found a cab standing right outside. "Hackney. And please step on it," said Darren to the cab driver. The cab raced through the empty streets of London, and time came to a standstill for Darren. He was on his way home. It took the cab twenty minutes to reach his home. Darren ran up the steps, not wanting to wait for the lift. He wanted to be home. He wanted to feel safe. He wanted to know it was over. He entered his home. It was exactly how he left it. He shut the door behind him and locked it. He made his way to the window, sat down on his chair, cracked the window open a bit, made himself a quick rollie, and lit it. He took a deep puff and released the smoke slowly.

"Fuck!" said Darren. It was over. It was finally over. But it wasn't quite over. He needed to hide the money. He opened the duffel bag to make sure the money was still there. He picked up the bag and made his way to the closet. He was about to keep the bag in when the main door swung open. Darren dropped the bag and out fell some of the money and jewellery from the bag. He took out his gun and pointed it at the man who had just entered.

The mysterious man was a short, fair man with no facial hair in sight. It was his best friend and fellow gang member, Bob. On closer inspection, Darren noticed that Bob had blood all over his black coat and a duffel bag of his own in his hand.

"Darren. It's me, Bob. Your mate." Bob looked at Darren's duffel bag full of money. "I'm in trouble. I need your help."

CHAPTER 6

BACK TO THE FUTURE PRESENT

The single bare lightbulb still dangled from the ceiling. The halo seemed less interesting now. Darren had reminisced enough. He wanted to paw at the lightbulb and make its halo sway about. But mostly, he just wanted to take his money and leave. He wanted to get far, far away. And he wanted to take Judy with him. And maybe his mum as well. The waiting was getting to him. And Bob wouldn't say a word about what happened to him. That added to the mystery. Darren hated mysteries. Except for Scooby-Doo.

Bob had entered Darren's flat covered in blood. Not his own blood. Someone else's blood. They had all asked Bob whose blood it was. He didn't say. He was shaking uncontrollably. And he kept asking them for a drink. They got worried and asked him again. He still kept asking for a drink. So they gave him one. It looked good so they all had one. He was still shaken. The rest were still worried. But also remarkably mellow. The gang had good taste when it came to whisky.

But the mellowness was skin deep. There were pressing questions that needed immediate answers. And no amount of whisky could make them go away. How did everyone end up with a duffel bag full of money and gold? It was more than a coincidence. This was planned. And it was planned quite well. And executed almost perfectly. Almost. Bob was the outlier. Drenched in another's blood. What led to this? What happened that made a once cheerful man go so sombre? The biggest question, however, was how Darren got paid double. Darren was hoping that it might get lost in the shuffle and search for other answers. It didn't.

It had been almost an hour and Bob hadn't said anything. Patience was running thin, especially for Riley who was the youngest of the group. Brash, cocky, dishonest, and an Arsenal fan were just some of the horrible words used to describe him. He had had way too many drinks already, and it became clear that he might just act out. He turns to Bob who was much older than the rest and bluntly says, "Tell us what happened to you mate, before we get too drunk to care. We've all just got a huge payday. I'm planning on getting fucked if you don't mind? And your moping is getting in the way. So out with it, old man. What's got you sobbing like a schoolgirl Sally who's just had her first real heartbreak?"

Dave felt the tension and quickly chimed in. "The pup might be a cunt, but he is right," and pours himself another drink. "You'd best let us know, Bobby, ole boy. Seeing how we could probably help you get out of a jam better than anyone else. You called us, and we're here. Just for you."

Bob looks at all of them and knows they are right. He downs his drink and begins to gather the courage to speak.

"I'm sorry it's taken me so long to open my mouth. But what happened earlier today was a lot to take in. And seeing all of you with your duffel bags full of money just like me made me think things over and over again in my head. It's become crystal clear that all of us had jobs today that we didn't tell the others about. The pay was way too good and we all got greedy. Or scared."

This had everyone's attention. They were all haunted by the same feeling.

Bob continues. "I wouldn't have sought out Darren and the rest of you if everything went swimmingly, which it clearly didn't. But I prefer calling this a blessing. Because it brought all of us here together tonight. We've all clearly gotten a very nice windfall, but this amount of money tends to draw a lot of attention. Mostly the bad kind. So we need to look out for each other and stay vigilant. Let's start by telling each other what we all did tonight. What were our jobs? So we can make sense of all of this."

There was a chorus of approval from all three of them.

Bob continues, "Let's start simple. Who offered you guys the job?"

"Some theatrical cunt who called himself Mr Shadow," says Dave.

Riley nods furiously. "That's the same guy who hired me. He was a tall and thin prick. Kinda like Darren."

"What do you mean, kinda like me?" Darren barks back and shoves Riley a bit. He didn't mean to be this aggressive but was. Maybe he was just cranky. He stops himself immediately.

"I didn't mean to upset you, mate," says Riley, trying to calm Darren down. "Have another drink." Darren was not someone you wanted to pick a fight with.

Darren calms himself down immediately and takes Riley's advice. He pours himself another drink, a stiffer one, and lights a spliff. "I was also hired by Mr Shadow. And Riley's description is spot on. Didn't get a good look at his face though. He made sure I didn't."

"Neither could I," adds Bob.

"Nor me," says Dave.

Riley just nods in agreement and takes the spliff from Darren.

"Spooky. But at least things are falling into place," says Bob. "Now we need to know what the jobs were that we did tonight at the behest of Mr Shadow. What did he plan in his night of the four crimes?"

Dave interjects, "Night of the four crimes. I like the way it sounds. It's like the title for some mystery novel. Let the next chapter be my story. So there I was..."

—X—

—— CHAPTER 7 ——

DAVE'S EXCELLENT ADVENTURE

Dave was walking down a suburban neighbourhood road wearing a thick coat and carrying a duffel bag. There was no one in sight. He checked his watch. It was 11.30 pm. *Everyone's asleep or having a wank*, he thought to himself. He walked past a lovely classic black sedan and slowed down just enough to admire it. He continued walking ahead and then swiftly unbuttoned his coat. Quietly, he slipped behind some dumpsters and re-emerged wearing a bandit hat and holding a long thin metal ruler with a hook at the end.

He rushed back to the classic black sedan swiftly and noiselessly. Dave was portly but unbelievably nimble in his movements. He took a good look at the car and its interiors. He then took the metal rod and hook and inserted it into the window slot. Jiggled it around a bit like he was looking for the clit and managed to find it. The mechanism to open the door, I mean. It worked like it was supposed to, and the door swings open. Dave couldn't help but smirk, but it was mostly because the car didn't have an alarm system.

It was a classic for sure with an ageless design. And easy to steal if you wanted to commit a crime. He sat inside and shut the car door. Didn't take his coat off.

What he does take off is the plastic shell below the steering wheel. He puts a small flashlight in his mouth to take a better look at the exposed wiring under the steering wheel. He then takes out a Swiss Army knife from his pocket and cuts some wires. He joins 2 wires to make a spark like they show in the movies. The car turns on; also just like in the movies. He adjusts the seat, rearview mirror and turns on the radio. It comes on blast playing some adult contemporary. "Fuck!" yells Dave as expected. "I love this song." continues Dave, which wasn't as expected. He told the fellas he listens to Metallica. He drives off with the car singing as soulfully as he could (not very).

About twenty minutes later, he turns the car into a narrow lane. Brings it to a screeching halt and parks it sideways, blocking the access to the lane from an intersection. He gets out of the car, leaving behind a trail of candy wrappers, and starts running away as fast as he could. He crosses some high-end fashion stores, one of them belonged to the hottest new designer in town, Louie James.

But if you asked Dave, he considered that cupcake overrated and overpriced. Dave also considered trackies and jumpers to be the height of fashion, but that was a discussion for another time. While Dave's movements were nimble for a portly man, his stamina was what you'd expect. Non-existent. He started getting shortness of breath after barely twenty steps. He trips and falls down on the ground. He crawls a bit and grabs onto the pole of a street lamp. Pulls himself up using the last bit of strength he had. "Please, God. Please help me." Unlike Darren, Dave believed in God. And his belief was rewarded. For God had answered. A black cab was coming his way, the only other car in his sight. He held out his hand to call it. It stopped right in front of him. The light from the street lamp hit the cab and made it look like it had a halo. "My guardian angel," mutters Dave and gets in the cab. It speeds off into the distance before stopping for a light and then making a sharp U-turn.

The black cab stopped in front of a large bungalow that looked like it belonged in a posh neighbourhood. And it did. Dave was somewhere in Chelsea. He noticed the car in the driveway had all its tyres punctured. *Fucking shame*, he thinks to himself in passing and walks past it.

He notices it has a peculiar bumper sticker on the rear windshield. He doesn't know what to make of it so gets back to the job at hand. He reaches the front door and makes short work of it. Pries it open with a crowbar.

Once inside, he ran up the stairs and went straight into the master bedroom. It had a sultan's bed with purple satin bedsheets. The rest of the room was a mix of furniture and furnishings that were definitely not from IKEA. This was the fancy stuff. The furniture was made from actual wood. Dave always had a snarky comment for everything, but the opulence of the room shut him up. This bothered him more than it should have. It gave him a bit of an upset tummy, and he let out a tiny fart. He clutched at his rotund globular mass to make himself feel better, but it had the opposite effect. All he could picture was a turtle emerging from its shell. "Fuck!" he yelled out louder than he should. He ran into the en suite washroom.

"Emerges a few minutes later, fresh and at ease.

Thoroughly search the room, just like a thief.

Finds nothing of value, oh no, it cannot be.

For Mr. Shadow had promised him more cash than he could dream."

Dejected and defeated, Dave stumbles face-first onto the bed. Turns himself over onto the pillow and stares at the ceiling blankly. "If I were a sultan, where would I hide my cash?" And then it hits him. He realises the only place he hadn't checked in the room. He jumps off the bed and lifts up the mattress. There was nothing underneath it. Just the firm thick wooden bed frame. But he knew something was amiss. He touches the underside of the mattress. Takes out his Swiss Army knife and tears it from the underside. Bundles of cash fall out from it. "More cash than he could dream." It just barely fits into his duffel bag. He had to pocket a few bundles in his coat.

Once he was done, he takes a good long look at the room and lights a cigarette. He coughs a bit and then a lot more after taking a few puffs. "Fuck, I hate these cancer sticks." He chucks the cigarette in a trash bin full of paper and it catches fire. It begins spreading beyond it onto the other parts of the room. It probably all eventually went kaboom!

"And then I was off. A simple job with very good pay," says Dave to the rest.

"What time did you reach the house?" inquires Riley, who was suddenly a lot more interested.

"I'd say about quarter to one," replies Dave.

"Very interesting," says Riley. He prods deeper, "What was the colour of the car out in the driveway?"

"Fancy navy-blue coloured sedan. I think it was a Benz," came the response.

Riley further asks, "Did it have a bumper sticker on the back that read…"

"Fishnets catch more than one kind of fish," both Riley and Dave say in unison.

This had everyone's attention. Even Darren looked less sleepy and more inclined to see this through. He poured himself another drink and lit another spliff. He was in this for the long haul now. Running away with Judy would have to wait until tomorrow. Maybe the day after tomorrow because tomorrow was Saturday. That meant karaoke night at his favourite bar, The Captain and the Nymph. He wowed audiences last month with his rendition of The Stone Roses classic "This is the One." He had been chasing that high ever since. Back to the story now.

"It's definitely the same car," adds Bob. "What time did you slash the tyres?" he asks Riley.

Riley thinks about it deeply but luckily not for long. "Around midnight, I think."

"Then what happened?" asks Bob.

CHAPTER 8

RILEY'S WILY TIME

Riley slashes the tyres of the sedan. He cowers behind it to make sure no one heard or saw anything. The sky was clear and so was the coast, so he puts his knife away. Getting out of there quietly and without being seen was paramount. He was still a few minutes away from his getaway vehicle. Cowed and bent, he hides behind different cars and obstructions to stay out of sight as much as possible.

A few minutes of this and he emerges at a proper intersection. It was late, but some chicken and chip shops were still open. Around them buzzed swarms of drunkards and the occasional group of Turkish men. Both sets of people were equally loud and arguing over the same thing. Whose football team is better? It didn't look like any of those arguments would be ending soon.

Riley turns around a corner into a small alley where he had parked his motorcycle. It was a heavily modded dirt bike that looked like it could climb a mountain. It also had a bicycle bell which made Riley giddy. What he really wanted to add to it though was a proper second seat. Darren told him not to bother because no one wanted to ride with him anyway. Riley called him a cunt and went on dreaming about the day he'd add that second seat. "If this job pays as much as promised I'll buy a new bike for every day of the week," he told himself and got on the bike. He rubbed the fuel tank lovingly, called the bike Joanna and rode off.

He stopped twenty minutes later in front of a corner office building that looked like a brick fortress and had no sign. He hid himself in an alley opposite it. He put on a pair of earphones and blasted some Libertines into his ears. He couldn't hear anything else around him. But he kept his eyes wide open looking right at the office. He took out a half-smoked spliff and lit it up.

He was about halfway through "Up the Bracket" when he saw a man in a bandit hat and a duffel bag exiting the place.

"Wait! Was this in Holborn?" Darren interjects and stops Riley's narration.

"God damn it, man! You're ruining my flow of storytelling. It stops being interesting if you're taken out of the moment," bites back Riley.

"I'm sorry, man. I really, really am." And he really was sorry. "But was this in Holborn?" Just not sorry enough to not ask again.

"Yes, it was. Pipe down now and let me tell the rest of my story," answered Riley, annoyed.

"That was me who you saw, by the way," says Darren, trying to have the last word. And it worked. It had everyone's attention. But Darren had nothing else to add. However, he needed to. They were all staring at him now.

"I had to break open a safe," he adds, hoping it would take the attention away from him. It didn't. "What did you do once I left?" he asks Riley, and it works. All eyes were on Riley now, not him.

Riley watched Darren leave the office building and kept a close eye on him until he was eventually out of sight. Then he went to the office door. It was still open. Riley reached inside his backpack and took out a manila envelope similar to the one Mr Shadow had given Darren. He rummaged inside and took out a heavy padlock. He used it to lock the door and walked back to his motorcycle. He mounted Joanna and rode off on her while chucking the key somewhere en route to his next destination.

Which happened to be in West Kensington in front of an upper-middle-class building that had seen better days. He takes a good look at it and parks his motorcycle on the side of it next to a large skip bin. He checks his Shrek themed watch and remarks, "I'm on time." He still had a bit of his spliff left and thought that this was as good a time as any. He puts the spliff in his mouth and takes out his lighter. He is about to spark it when it slips from his hands and falls on the floor, breaking.

THUD! It sounded a lot louder than it should have. A startled Riley took out his knife and looked around. There was no one. But what was that sound? It couldn't have been the lighter. Turned around and saw that someone had dropped something into the skip bin from one of the higher floors. He went to see what it was. It was a duffel bag. Just as it was promised by Mr Shadow. He looked around to make sure no one else is there. There wasn't. He was alone. And it was quiet. So quiet that he could hear was his heartbeat, and it was pounding like a marching drum. He was almost scared to open the bag. What if it's not what he was promised? Then what? He didn't have an answer for that. But what if it was exactly what was promised? Either way, he knew he had to open it.

He opens the bag with his eyes tightly shut. He slowly opens them and lets his vision come back into focus. Once it did, he had to rub his eyes to make sure that this wasn't an illusion. It wasn't. In fact, it was everything he could have wished for. Oodles of cash and jewellery. Everything that was promised and more. He shuts the bag quickly and takes another look around. He couldn't see anyone, but that didn't make him feel any safer. Just more exposed. And alone. He gets on his bike without wasting another moment and rides away.

"And then I got a call to come here and meet with you soy boy cunts," says Riley, finishing his story. "Not what I'd call a difficult job, but who am I to complain. I got what I wanted. The only other thing I want now is another drink and what do we have here." Riley picks up the whisky bottle, pours all of it into his glass, and adds some water. In a pinch, Bob picks up the glass, finishes the drink, and slams the glass hard on the table before Riley could object.

"I was the one who threw that duffel bag down, pup. And up till then everything was perfect, my world was at peace. If only I could go back and do it all differently."

"Do what differently?" asks Darren. Bob doesn't answer. Keeps reminiscing and shaking his head in disbelief. "Do what differently?" asks Darren again, this time louder. Bob looks at him and begins to speak.

—— CHAPTER 9 ——

BOB'S JOB

Bob was standing in front of the Upper-Middle-Class West Kensington building that had seen better days. But in his eyes, it looked perfect. Age gave it character, much like it did to him. Or so he hoped. "If this job pays as well as it promises, I could probably live in a building like this. Not have to do another job ever again," he thought to himself. "Be a well-respected man, living with a plan, being given a second chance, oh boy I could dance." He daydreamed some more. But it was too late to be daydreaming. At this time, most people were regular dreaming. Still, the thought didn't stop him from having a smile on his face and a spring in his step.

The spring in his step pushed him forward towards the building and the job. Every job brought with it some bit of unease and anxiety for Bob. But not this time. He just felt confident. He had decided that this was going to be the last job he'd ever do. After this, it was going to be nothing but peace and quiet. The simple life. The daydreaming wasn't going to stop. He reached the entrance and punched in the security key code. He had memorised it. Just like a resident. Like someone who belonged.

Once inside, he walked down to the end of the hallway to the lift. It was right there waiting for him. It opened slowly as he entered quickly and pushed all the right buttons. He waited patiently for the lift door to shut, but it was taking its sweet time. He pushed the lift close button, but nothing happened. He pushed it repeatedly, but the door still didn't shut. It was turning into a frustrating ordeal.

The main door of the building opens. In entered one of the residents; this pale, tall and lithe man who had had more drinks than he should have, but if you mentioned it to him he would have politely disagreed with you. And then would have chatted for 10 more minutes about the most inane and puerile things. Definitely someone you'd want to avoid as a neighbour. And Bob wanted to avoid everyone. He was on a job. He didn't want to be seen by anyone. He wanted to be forgotten.

The drunk man looks towards the lift and calls out to Bob, "Please hold it." Bob nodded and smiled but keeps pushing the door close button. It made no difference. The lift door was stuck.

And so was Bob. He accidentally pushed the door open button and it finally begins to close. The buttons were reversed! Bob pretends as if he has no control of the lift and is trying his best to keep the door open. The lift door had almost shut. Bob had almost made it. I use the word 'almost' because the drunk man ran and was able to jam his hand in at the last moment. The lift door opened up again, allowing the drunk man to enter.

Bob nodded at him and tried his best not to draw any undue attention to himself. The drunk man looks at the floor buttons and smiles. Turned to Bob. "Looks like we're going on the same floor. Hello, floor buddy. Haven't seen you around. Who are you? Just moved in? You look like a family man with a bunch of rugrats running around."

Bob smiled back nervously. A thousand thoughts raced through his mind on how to deal with him. The problem was almost all of them were illegal, time-consuming, and attention-drawing. "I'm visiting some family." He drew the drunk's attention to the duffel bag he's carrying. "Got into town earlier today. Had some work to do so just checking in."

"That's wonderful," replied the drunk man. "Which one of my lovely neighbours are you related to, if you don't mind me asking? I'd wager a guess, but that could turn out badly. It's Carol, isn't it?"

Bob was cornered. He didn't like being cornered. His first instinct was to punch the drunk man and knock him out. But Bob had learned never to follow his instinct. That's what landed him in prison for 10 years. "I'm sorry, who are you?" Bob asks the drunk man, wanting him to talk instead.

The drunk man looked like he was about to break into a song and dance about himself when the lift door opened and it startled him a bit. This was a good enough distraction for Bob to be on his way. "Goodnight. Hope to see you in the morning and continue this lovely chat."

"Yes, I do hope so. Goodnight, fine sir." replied the drunk man.

Bob rushed past him to the flat he was instructed to go to. The drunk man followed him. Bob began clenching his fists for a punch. There was that instinct kicking in. Turned out the drunk man lived right opposite the flat Bob had his job in. He smiled and pretended to look for his keys. The drunk man opened his door and turned to Bob. "So you're related to Anthony? He's a fine upstanding gentleman. To be honest, you guys don't look related."

"He's my wife's cousin," says Bob.

"You don't say. Well, we'll pick this conversation up in the morning. Probably with Mr Anthony present as well. Goodnight, sir." The drunk man said this and stumbled inside his flat.

"Good night. Take care." Bob said and waited for the drunk man's door to shut. He waited a moment to make sure everything is settled and there are no more distractions. The drunk man started blaring some loud dance music. *That'll keep him occupied*, Bob thought to himself and turned his attention to the door of the flat he was supposed to enter. He took out a small pocket-sized set of tools to break in. He inserted a pin into the keyhole but realised the door is unlocked. Could he be that lucky? Or was it a setup? Bob hoped it was the first option but prepares for the second option. He took out a small pistol from his pocket, a little something provided by Mr Shadow. "Could be needed," he said, all the while Bob hoped he didn't.

He entered the room quietly and closed the door behind him as softly as possible. The flat was silent. But it didn't mean it was empty. Bob's gut told him it wasn't. "There is someone else here," he told himself. He took out a tiny flashlight to look around and saw a man sitting on a chair right in front of him. He screamed and dropped his flashlight. The man doesn't move or say a word.

Bob picks up the flashlight to take a better look at the man. One proper look made it clear that he wasn't ever going to move or speak again. Shot on the forehead, execution style. But before that, he was tied up and tortured. And the wounds were fresh. But the blood hadn't splattered. It was contained. *Thoroughly professional work*, Bob thought to himself and felt unsettled. And not just because it wasn't a pretty sight. *Whoever did this could still be around*. He decided to cover the windows and take a quick look around the home. There was no one else luckily. Just him and the dead man. And with the dead man, he waited.

About twenty minutes later, Bob heard someone walking outside in the hallway. "Could be needed," he remembered Mr Shadow's words as he drew his gun again and points it at the door. The person outside was now standing right in front of the flat door. "Who could it be?" wondered Bob over and over again with only one answer coming to mind. *"The professional. Maybe his forehead would be next?"*

The person outside slipped something made of metal under the door and began to walk away. Bob heard the footsteps ebbing into the distance. He ran to the door to see what was slid under it. It was a golden key. Beautifully crafted with its bow looking like a rosebud. Bob turned his attention to the person who slid it. He was curious to know who it was. He opened the flat door and peeked towards the lift. Its door was just closing, and he saw a brief glimpse of the man who had slid the key. He was a tall and lithe man in all black carrying a duffel bag. He couldn't make out his face. *"Mr Shadow!"* Bob thought to himself.

"Was this in West Kensington?" interjects Darren.

"Fucking hell! What is it with you and cutting the flow of the story? Do you have to interrupt at the best parts?" an irate Riley asks Darren.

"I'm sorry. I didn't mean to interrupt," Darren says apologetically. "But was this in West Ken?" Darren asks Bob again unironically.

"It was," replies Bob.

"That was me again," says Darren. "I slid the key under the door. I was asked to by Mr you-know-who. And I remember someone peeking out when I was in the lift."

"So it wasn't Mr. Shadow in the lift?" asks Bob.

"Listen to what I'm saying, it was me. And I remember that key. Gold with a bow that looked like a rosebud," Darren replies.

"So it was you I saw in the lift. Kind of anticlimactic," says a puzzled Bob.

"But where did the blood come from?" interjects Dave. He had had enough of distractions during story time.

"And when did you throw the duffel bag? Did you know what was in it?" asks Riley, which adds to the list of unanswered questions they wanted answers for.

Bob recalls watching the elevator shut, taking Darren down. He softly closed the door of the flat. Took a better look at the key. He knew just where this would fit. He figured it out when he did a sweep of the place earlier. He went to the beautiful cabinet in the master bedroom. It was made of thick wood and clad with marble. It was bulletproof and nearly impossible to break into.

The key fit perfectly and it unlocked with a satisfying sound. He opened it and found it packed with cash and gold. Bob had never seen this much money together in real life. Neither had the other gang members, but Bob was older by almost a decade. So this was a long time coming. *I could just run away with all of it,* Bob thought to himself. But then he remembered what Mr Shadow had said. "Follow my instructions to the T, or I'll kill you in the most unimaginable way imaginable." Those words stuck with him and snapped him back to reality.

He took out a duffel bag from within his duffel bag. Divided the money and gold in half, just as he was instructed to. It took him almost twenty minutes to do so. He wanted it to be exact. He checked the time. It was 2.10 am. It was time. He picked up one bag, opened the kitchen window, and threw it down without looking. It made a loud thud sound, but that was not his concern. He did what Mr Shadow had asked. Nothing more and nothing less.

He picked up the receiver of the landline. Dialled a number and lets it ring off the hook. "That was the last thing on the checklist," Bob realises this and can't help but smile. He picked up his duffel bag to be on his way. It was time to end his final job ever. This brought a tear to his eyes. But he realised one thing. He wasn't going to miss this line of work. He was happy to be done. He was wiping his hands clean.

He went to the main door and turns around to take one last look at the flat. Made sure he hasn't left anything behind. Opened the door and is surprised to see the drunk man from before standing right outside the door about to ring the doorbell.

"I'm sorry I didn't mean to startle you. I just wanted to borrow some sugar for some tea," the drunk man says. "If I could just squeeze in?" The drunk man tried to enter the flat.

Bob stopped him. "I'm sorry. This isn't a good time."

The drunk man protests. "I just want some sugar. Anthony takes whatever he likes from my kitchen. And I'm accorded the same privileges. Now please step aside." The drunk man pushed Bob aside and entered. It was dark, but the hallway let some light seep in. Enough for the drunk man to see the dead man tied to the chair. He walks a few steps ahead to take a better look.

"Anthony! What have you done to Anthony?" the drunk man yells loudly. This was going to draw unwanted attention. It wouldn't be long before the rest of the neighbours would join them. And the drunk man had seen his face. And now he wouldn't forget it. This was the last job Bob was supposed to do. But not for these reasons. This was supposed to be his happy ending. Soon the fuzz would arrive and put him back in prison. He didn't want to go back to prison. He couldn't go. Especially after what had happened the last time. Over and over and against his will. No! No! He could not go back in there. He didn't like the way he was being cornered. He didn't like being cornered.

Everything fell out of focus. The drunk man's screaming was tuned out. Bob didn't know what to do. But he had to do something. He needed to do something. He was going to do something. He was going to let his instinct take over. BANG! He whipped out his pistol and shot the drunk man behind his head. His body ricocheted forwards and falls face-first into Anthony's crotch.

The witness was dealt with. But it wasn't over yet. The gunshot would have been heard half a block away. And they'll all be looking over here. Too many prying eyes. He had to run. He drops the gun on the floor and dashes away. One of the neighbours, a middle-aged woman, had come out to see what had happened. Bob tackled her before she could take a proper look at him. He runs down the stairs before anyone else stepped out of their homes.

Once outside, he turned around to take a look. A group of people had gathered around the bodies. A few of them saw him running away. "But they haven't seen my face," Bob reassured himself as he heard sirens in the distance.

"But they hadn't seen my face," Bob says, hoping the guys would reassure him.

Dave gets up and puts his hand on Bob's shoulder. "I don't know what you're going through. It can't be easy. I won't pretend to understand. I've never had to kill a man. I don't think any of us have." Darren looks away. He didn't want anyone to see his eyes. Dave continues. "The only advice I can give is to get rid of the clothes and try to stay out of sight until the heat subsides. We'll take care of this. But for now, it's late. We all should get some rest. Deal with this with a fresh set of eyes and a fresh mind."

Bob nods and shakes Dave's hand. "Thanks, Dave. Get some rest. All of you should."

Riley also shakes Bob's hand. "Take care, mate. See you on the morrow. Don't worry too much about what's happened. You did what you had to, and I don't blame you." Turns to Dave. "Drop me off, mate? Don't want to take my duffel bag on Joanna. Had too much of the sauce." Dave agrees.

"All right boys. We're off. We'll figure this out tomorrow. We'll figure out who this Mr Shadow is. We'll figure out what he wants from us. And most importantly, we'll figure out why Darren got paid double." says Dave and starts to laugh.

His laughter caused pangs of pain in Darren's head. He also had had too much to drink. But also not enough to drown out all the noise in his head. He had a complicated relationship with alcohol. And reality in general.

"Maybe Darren sucked him off." adds Riley charmingly as ever. Dave starts laughing even more loudly. Darren's headache grows larger. Even Bob joins in with a snicker.

Darren was now fuming inside. He tried to mount a defence but couldn't. That made him even more grumpy. But he had to say something. Then it hit him. He had the perfect comeback. It brought a devilish smile to his face. And he was ready to drop it.

"Alright, everyone. Goodbye." says Dave before Darren could use his comeback.

Darren clenches his fist tightly but shows no emotion on his face. "Good night, mates. See you tomorrow."

Dave and Riley head out, leaving Darren and Bob behind. Darren walks towards Bob and holds his hand out to him.

"I guess you're also heading home?" says Bob.

"No! I was going to say that we should go back to your place to have a few more drinks since the dead weights are gone. We need to celebrate! We're millionaires now," replies Darren.

Bob looks up to him from his chair and smiles. They leave their hideout, a flat in Tower Hamlets they'd been squatting in.

—X—

—— CHAPTER 10 ——

THICKENING OF THE PLOT

The bulb hanging in Bob's living room had a china-ball on it. It helped spread the light evenly across the room, giving it a cosy and family-friendly atmosphere. It was like a basic cable American sitcom. Darren wanted to tell a joke to see if he'd hear any laughter. But to whom would he tell a joke? Bob was in the kitchen for what seemed like forever. But Darren didn't mind. Bob was getting beer and crisps. Darren loved beer and crisps. It was the only thing that was going to keep him from falling asleep.

It was quite late and all Darren wanted to do was wrap himself up like a burrito in his quilt. Sleep for a day or two at least. But all that had to wait. He needed to be here. He needed to be here for Bob. He met Bob in prison. His first and only friend in there. Bob defended him when no one would. And he defended Bob more than he could. When they were released, Darren had a chance encounter with Dave and Riley. The three of them went to school together but weren't the thickest of mates back then. Dave had just left his

Tower Hamlets crew and worked odd jobs with Riley, who was still green. A night of drinking and reminiscing about sixth form was all it took for the three of them to decide to work together. But after an odd job or two, they knew something was off. They needed one more man in their crew. Darren then introduced Bob to Dave and Riley. That's when the gang came into being. Bob taught them so many skills of the trade. Taught them how to be better thieves. Taught them how to keep calm on a job and not let instinct dictate how things would go. All this Darren would learn during their first heist together, a TV store on Regent Street. Bob detected a secret alarm none of them had seen and disabled it before it went off. It was moments like this that made one thing clear. Bob was their leader. Not just because he was older but because he was also a lot smarter and bolder. Age had given him wisdom they still lacked. But most importantly Bob was like their elder brother. Someone they could rely on. So no, Darren couldn't leave. Not yet. Not till Bob was at peace. Sleep would have to wait for a few hours more.

Bob entered the living room carrying with him a large ice bucket packed with beer cans and a family-sized packet of Walkers crisps. Darren preferred

Kettle, but Walkers would do. Darren grabs the ice bucket from Bob, places it at a convenient spot, and hands Bob and himself a nice cold "brewski". Imagining himself say that word made Darren feel dirty. Judy was rubbing too much American on him. And he was a proud East Londoner. They both crack open a cold one, smashed 'em for cheers, gulped most of it down in one go, and simultaneously let out a disgusting burp.

"H A H A H A H A H A H A H A H A H A H A H A H H A HAHAHAHAHA!" They were surrounded by laughter. Darren's nightmare had come true. He had walked into a sitcom. He frantically looked around for the cameras and the audience. Only a second later, he realised that it was the next-door neighbours watching "Mock the Week" reruns.

"You know I've been thinking," says Bob, snapping Darren out of his fantasy and into grim reality.

"Come on, Bob-o. You promised me on the way here that you'd take it easy. You've had a difficult night," interrupts Darren and makes his way right next to Bob. He puts his arm around Bob's shoulder and softly whispers, "You had to kill someone. That can't be easy to live with. I can't imagine what you're going through," Darren lies easily.

Bob was quite surprised at this outburst by Darren. It even made Darren think if he overdid it. "I was just going to say that I've been thinking of getting a nice new settee. Maybe a pull-out," Bob meekly replies. "What do you think?"

Darren did overreact. But his heart was in the right place. Plus, he was too drunk to give solid advice. He could listen, though. Maybe that's all Bob needs. Someone to listen to. And he was not letting Bob unburden himself. That's not cool. He's being a bad friend. A bad, bad friend. He deserved to be spanked right now. His thoughts had drifted again towards Judy.

"Look, mate. I know you want to talk about earlier tonight," says Darren. "If talking will help you feel lighter, then I'm all ears."

Bob was genuinely touched by this gesture.

"But only till the beer lasts. So you better hurry," adds Darren and finishes his first beer. Cracks open a second one.

Bob smiles a bit and shakes his head in acceptance. "Thanks, mate. Means a lot to me. The thing that's been picking on my mind is what's in it for Mr Shadow?"

"What do you mean?" asks a confused Darren.

Bob continues. "From what I understand, all four of us were hired by him to commit different crimes in different parts of the city, which are all interconnected in some way. The plan is near perfect and helps all four of us become very rich men. That leads me to have one question in my mind. Which is…" Bob points at Darren, wanting him to answer.

"What's in it for him?" replies Darren, understanding.

"Exactly!" Bob replies. "From what I piece together, he gets no money, no item of intrinsic or emotional value."

"Intrinsic?"

Bob continues. "Now, why were certain actions asked to be performed? I was made to babysit a flat with 2 million inside and had to wait for you to give me the key. What else did I have to do?

"Make a phone call and then leave it off the hook," Darren answers as if it's a quiz.

"Which lets the caller know who it is but can't call back. What would you do if someone important to you made a call like that in the middle of the night?" asks Bob.

"I'd rush over," comes Darren's reply.

"And I'm guessing that guy did too. And what would he find?"

"A dead body tied to a chair. And a safe that's been broken into."

"That man was killed maybe an hour before I reached that flat. He hadn't started rotting. And he was killed with clean, precise gunshots. This leads to another question. Who killed him?"

Darren thinks about it deeply. But luckily not for long. "Mr Shadow?" he inquires instead of answering.

"Maybe. But when you broke into the office you had to rob, what did you find there?"

"A dead guy on the assistant's table," Darren replies meekly.

"Did you notice anything particular about him?" inquires Bob.

"He was a fresh kill. Hadn't rotted. Had clean, precise gunshots," Darren says, finally realising what Bob was trying to get at. "Could they be done by the same person?"

"Maybe! But they are connected for sure. Now another question. The guy I called probably rushed over to that flat late at night, but where was he coming from?"

"It was late. Probably home," Darren answers with confidence.

"I thought so too. But then when you take Riley's job into consideration, it gets tricky. He had to go and slash the tyres of a car, hardly 10 minutes before you break into an office which I'm guessing had some kind of alarm system."

"Probably. No one showed up, though."

"Now, assume the alarm went off. He gets ready and storms out only to find his car tyres have been slashed. What would he do next?"

"Probably get a cab."

Bob takes out a map of London. "Now, judging from where this guy lives and where he works, the quickest way to reach it is by a small lane here" (while pointing at the map) "which, ironically, was..."

Darren interjects. "Blocked by a stolen sedan. The one Dave stole." His eyes had lit up. "So he had to turn around and take a whole different route to get there."

Bob adds to the clamour. "You found the office unlocked, but Riley locked it and disposed of the key."

"So when he reaches there but finds it locked. But when he enters, he finds out that not only has he been robbed of 2 million in cash and gold but his assistant is also dead." Darren says, realising.

"It's also around the same time I made the call and left the phone off the hook," Bob tells Darren. "Now what does he do? He rushes to West Ken to meet someone he trusts with 2 million pounds of his. This is someone close. Business partner, brother, best friend or lover."

"Only to find him tied to a chair and shot dead. Along with the neighbour you had to take out," Darren adds.

Bob felt a little uneasy remembering the fact he killed someone. "And also he'll find the 2 million quid missing," Bob says, trying to shift the focus from the dead neighbour. "Talk about a rough night. But it doesn't end there."

Darren remembers the rest of Dave's job. "Dave stole the money from his home and set his house on fire."

"It's the ultimate 'fuck you'. You are out 5 million quid. Your lover and assistant have been killed. You get back home dealing with all of this to find the fire brigade trying to extinguish what's left of your house. A pretty elaborate plan for fucking over one person using us." Bob pauses and looks at Darren in the eye. "So tell me, mate. As far as Mr Shadow is concerned, what's in it for him?"

Darren had the answer on the tip of his tongue. It was all so clear now. "Revenge."

Bob smashes his beer can on the coffee table. "Exactly! Now we just need to know who Mr Shadow is and who he had us screw over."

Darren remembers the manila envelope Mr Shadow gave him. And the words he said when Darren realised it had a gun. "Inside the file are details of who you're stealing from. I'd keep a warm gun ready in my hand." But why didn't he tell the others? What was so special about him? Why did he get paid double? Well, if he was going to get answers to any of those questions, he's going to have to find Mr Shadow. And for that, he was going to need help.

"I know who we stole from," Darren tells Bob, who was clearly taken aback.

"Who?" asks Bob excitedly.

Darren looks Bob in the eyes and is about to tell him.

Bob interjects and shouts at him, "Wake the fuck up!"

Confuses Darren and rightfully so. "What?" he asks curiously.

"Wake the fuck up!" Bob shouts again, but this time he sounded like Judy. And he pinches him.

Darren wakes up startled, only to see Judy standing right in front of him with a cup of coffee in her hand. He looks around and sees he's on his bed. "What time is it?"

"After lunch, and yours has gone cold," Judy points at an unopened Chinese takeaway box.

Darren was still quite unsure about what was happening.

"How are you feeling now?" Judy asks him. Darren doesn't know what to say. "Are you still ill like last night?"

Darren remembers he had lied to her so he could do the job. What he couldn't remember was the rest of the night at Bob's and how he came back.

He should check up on him. They did drink a lot. But first, he wanted to have some of that Chinese food. He was hoping it was moo shu pork. Judy was still waiting for a response from him. "I'm feeling a lot better, love. Sleep was really all that I needed."

Judy smiles and kisses him. He liked that. He liked that very much. "We have to meet your mum tonight, I hope you remember," and hearing it made Darren remember. "You have ten missed calls from her among others. We're not cancelling again."

Dear old mum meeting his dearly beloved. This had to go well. It had to. "Yes, I remember, love. Looking forward to it very, very much," Darren says glibly.

And Judy notices this. "What's bothering you now?"

"I love her but she's a bit too much to handle."

"That's how all mothers are. Wait till you meet mine."

Darren knew there was no point arguing further. It was already decided.

And Judy knew this too. "Text me the plan when you have it all figured out."

"Yes, mum." He responds cheekily.

She looks at him, shakes her head and smiles. Gives him another kiss. He kisses her back passionately. He didn't want to stop kissing her. He wasn't going to stop kissing her. His phone begins to ring loudly. He puts it on silent without looking.

He lifts up Judy and almost throws her on the bed. Lies on top of her and continues kissing her. She kisses him back even more. Things were getting hot and heavy really fast, and there was nothing more important to Darren at this point in life right now. His phone begins to ring again loudly, so he throws it away. "There was nothing more important," he takes a good look at Judy, and he was sure of one thing. She was the one. He was never more sure of anything else in his life. And now he had the money to give her the life she deserves. He looks at her and smiles. She smiles back.

"What are you smiling about?" she tentatively asks him.

"I think at this moment in my life everything is perfect. And I hope it stays this way," Darren answers. His phone starts ringing again, and it kills the mood for him. "For fuck's sake! Let a man breathe."

"Pick it up, babe. It could be important," Judy suggests.

Darren picks up his phone and sees the screen has cracked. But he doesn't care. It was Dave. He answers the phone aggressively. "This better be a goddamn emergency!" He hears Dave's response from the other end and begins to look worried. "I'll be there. I'm leaving now."

— CHAPTER 11 —

What Do We Do Now?

Darren gulped a double espresso from a local coffee shop and took a black cab to Bob's. He was too hungover for the tube or, God forbid, the bus. He reached Bob's block of flats and started having flashbacks of last night. He looked over to the side and saw a wheelie bin. He vividly remembered throwing up in it. And then keeling over, falling on the ground and hurting his head. He touched the back of his head and it still had a slight bump. Darren hoped that he hadn't done anything else regrettable last night. He eyes some parked police vans nearby but doesn't think too much about them.

He makes his way up the building and onto Bob's floor. "Ding!" went the bell sound as the lift door opened and out came Darren. But what he saw made him impulsively take a step back. The hallway was full of cops. The "Po-Po". The Fuzz. This was not the place he wanted to be. And almost wasn't, but he stopped himself. Only because he saw Dave and Riley standing quietly in the corner. They looked distraught and helpless. But that was expected. Dave said on the phone, "Come to

Bob's. It's an emergency." What else did he expect to see? The police vans downstairs started to make sense. Darren was ready for the worst.

"What happened?" inquires Darren.

Riley broke into tears, and no amount of comforting from Dave was of any help. "Bob's dead! Someone killed him last night in his home."

Darren stood there without emotion. It wasn't like he wasn't sad. He was devastated. But to such a degree that his body didn't know how to react. It was as if his soul was kicked out of his own body. He was off the matrix. Off the grid. But he couldn't be. He had to take control.

"What happened? Where is he?" inquires Darren.

Dave points towards Bob's room while tending to Riley, who was still crying his heart out. Darren entered Bob's flat and watched it being turned inside out by the police forensic team. It no longer looked like a sitcom; it was more like a crime procedural show, still basic American cable. He saw the bedroom was sealed off, and the inspectors inside were taking pictures. But Darren got a peek at something he wished he hadn't.

He saw Bob lying on his bed motionless. But his eyes and mouth were wide open. He looked like he died in agonising pain. But that wasn't the whole story. He had also been shot several times in his legs. The lower half of his right arm had been cut off and was missing. And there was still more. He had marks all over his neck. He had been choked to death. No wonder his mouth was gaping open. He was gasping for air. Darren could imagine all of it happening but he didn't want to. Bob was killed in the most unimaginable way imaginable. That's another thought he didn't want in his head. All of this made Darren want to throw up. But he had to be strong. He had to endure this for all of them. He picks himself up and looks to enter the bedroom. No amount of cordoning off was going to stop him from taking a closer look.

"Please stay out. We're collecting evidence. And we still have to move the body," said one of the inspectors in the room.

"His name is Bob. Robert Wells," interjected Darren angrily but in pain. "And he was like my brother."

"I'm sorry for your loss, mate. I understand. I really do. But please wait outside. My partner, Inspector Melanie, will be with you and the others shortly. We have a few questions to ask," said the inspector politely. Darren took a good look at the inspector. He was a relatively young black man with greying hair. His name was Russel. He looked earnest and just wanted to do his job. So Darren calmed down, nodded, and did what he was told.

He made his way to the boys who were smoking cigarettes on the fire escape. Even Dave was sucking down on one, which he only ever did when he was pissed drunk or just devastated. Darren grabbed the cigarette pack from Riley, took one out with shaky hands, and looked for a light in his pockets. Dave handed him one, which Darren accepted with a smile. He lit the cigarette and walked a floor down, tucked himself into a corner away from all prying eyes, and broke down crying uncontrollably. And then it happened. He had the urge to throw up again. This time he did. He defaced most of a wall, but he didn't feel any better, just more miserable. He hadn't eaten a morsel of food since waking up, but he couldn't force himself to eat a bite at this moment. He wouldn't be able to keep it down. He just wanted to cry until he fell asleep again or wake up if this was some terrible nightmare.

"Darren! Come here!" Dave shouted from the floor above. Darren tossed his cigarette aside and stuffed his mouth with some mints. He wiped his tears and walked back to the boys. They had been joined by a young female redhead inspector.

"Hello, Darren, I presume. I'm Inspector Melanie. I have some questions to ask all of you. Please answer truthfully. It'll help us in finding the perpetrators who did this."

"Yes, Inspector. Ask away," says Dave.

"I'm sorry, Inspector. But before you do, we have a right to know what happened to our friend," interjects Darren harshly. He realises this and calms his tone. "Please, ma'am. We just want to know the truth."

Melanie took a look at Darren and believed him. "Well, your friend went through hell. Someone tortured him, maimed him, and then strangled him to death. Sometime between 6 and 7 this morning."

Darren couldn't remember where he was around that time. Was he at home? Did he just barely miss the killer? This revelation led to more questions in his head than answers.

"There's no sign of forced entry. And every clue suggests this is the work of professional. Someone who took time to torture your friend. Someone who enjoyed it very much. This makes us ask the question. Was your friend involved with someone dangerous? We've already checked and we know he's served time. So it's not impossible. In fact, it's probable."

"Not that we know of," replies Darren calmly. Inside, he was anything but that.

"Please think! This is no ordinary crime. Nothing was stolen. The TV, stereo, and other valuables are still here. We still don't know the motive. There's no unusual fingerprints, no hair strands, nothing. We're running some tests, but it'll take two or three days before we learn anything. If at all. Any clue or morsel of information can go a long way," says Inspector Melanie.

"And we will let you know, Inspector. But we don't know a damn thing!" answers Darren confidently. But it was clear he wanted this conversation to end.

"Alright. We'll be in touch. Please don't share details of this crime with anyone, especially the media. We've been given strict orders from up-top to keep it under wraps because of the severity of it all. We don't want to create a panic."

"We understand." Darren answers for the gang. Dave and Riley nod in agreement.

Inspector Melanie continues, "Someone from forensics will be with you shortly to take your fingerprints and DNA."

"Are we in trouble?" asks a scared Riley.

"It's standard procedure. We need to cross-check with whatever DNA we find inside. If you're innocent, you've got nothing to worry about. And in my experience, I've seen only very dumb criminals return to the scene of the crime," replies Melanie.

"Or extremely intelligent ones," says Darren.

"What do you mean?" asks Melanie.

"The other kind of criminal who would return to the scene of the crime," answers Darren.

"Right! Sure!" A confused Melanie responds. She doesn't know what to make of it. Neither did the boys. Darren wasn't feeling too confident about his answer now either. "I'll be on my way, gents. Good day," said Melanie and walks away.

The boys wait for her to be more than an earshot away and all turn to face each other.

"What do we do now?" asks a worried Dave.

—X—

CHAPTER 12

WHY THE ANTAGONISM?

A single bare lightbulb dangled from the ceiling. Its filament flickered from time to time. Darren had had enough of the flickering, so he took it out and replaced it with a new bulb. An LED energy saver. He stood on the rusted table, trusting it with his weight more than the shorter and leaner Riley would. He changed the light in a jiffy, and it made a world of difference. The light spread evenly across the room so they could get down to business.

"I honestly thought we got away with the perfect crime. Four interconnected plots in different parts of the city that were timed to perfection and performed by men who had no real motive. I guess I was just being naive," says Dave.

"It wasn't perfect. Bob had to kill someone to get away. There were witnesses all around," interjects Darren.

"So are you blaming him?" thunders Riley, slamming his fist on the table.

"NO!" shouts Darren, slamming the table even harder. It was one good hit away from falling apart. "What I'm saying is, someone probably saw him leaving the flat?"

"And told who?" asks Riley. "The coppers? I don't think they'd do that to him. And his share of the money is missing."

"Another thing that doesn't add up," adds Dave. "Why torture him if the money is already there? What's the point of it?"

"It's gotta be Mr Shadow. He said, 'I'll kill you in the most unimaginable way imaginable,'" answers Riley.

"And now he's going to come for us. And our money," remarks Dave.

"Let's not get paranoid over nothing," interjects Darren.

"Bob is dead! He was murdered. That is not nothing!" Yells Riley at the top of his voice.

"I never said it wasn't! He was my best fucking friend, damn it! And now he's dead! I want to find who did this, and I want to kill that fucking person with my bare hands, choking the life out of them!"

yells Darren even louder. Then he calms himself down. "But I prefer keeping my head cool in the process. And not do anything stupid like chase a delusional fantasy or a phantom of a man."

"Then what do you suggest?" asks Dave.

"Look, I know as much as you guys. I also think it is Mr Shadow. The circumstantial evidence falls on him. But we'll only know for sure once we find him. What we do know is that from the instructions he gave us, he did seem to know a lot about the victim. And he planned everything to perfection. Bob ruined his perfect plan, and he might have paid the price for it. And he paid for it dearly. I don't wish that on any of us. So we can't be rash and show him all our cards. We need to find him, and the only way we can do that is if we discuss everything we know about him," says Darren.

"But what do we know about him?" asks a puzzled Riley.

"He likes to wear black trench coats and hats," answers Dave.

"Well, so do I," says Darren. Dave and Riley notice he's wearing a long black trench coat, black military boots, and a hat. They look at him oddly. "A lot of people wear black."

"He likes to smoke cigars," says Dave.

"And drink whisky," adds Riley.

"We all love whisky. And cigars," says Darren.

"That's true," Dave and Riley say in unison.

"We could have some whisky while we discuss things over," suggests Riley.

Darren's body hadn't digested all the alcohol from yesterday. He still had a splitting headache and a dry cough. He had barely slept and hadn't eaten all day. It was easy to predict his answer. "Sure, Riles. Make mine a double."

Riley does what he's asked for happily. Makes a small drink for Dave as well. He knew Dave would come around and have it eventually. And he was right. Dave picked up his drink the second he saw Darren and Riley having a sip of theirs.

"A toast for Bob!" Dave suggests, followed by a few loud clanks in memory of their friend before getting back on topic.

"So we've got nothing on Mr Shadow," says Riley.

"We can't give up this quickly," replies Dave. "There's got to be something. How did you guys meet him?"

"In some small back alley space close to Hackney Market where he shone a light directly in my face from behind him. He was in complete silhouette like a shadow. Couldn't even get a good look at his face," answers Darren.

"Ditto!" adds Riley. "One thing's for sure. He was an odd man."

"Yeah, I agree. He seemed kind of warm in a weird way. And also threatening at the same time. If that makes sense?" says Darren.

"No, it doesn't," interjects Dave. "But nothing about this man does. When I met him, we had a small chat and then he gave me all the details in a manila envelope."

"Oh, the manila envelope!" sighs Riley.

"I don't know, but I kinda liked it. Makes the operation so much more professional. Like we work in an office or something like that," Darren explains with a proud smile on his face. "What was your meeting like with him, Riles? Anything particular you remember?"

"Pretty much word for word what you guys went through," answers Riley.

"But there's got to be something else," says Darren hopefully.

"There is actually," replies Dave. "You got paid double. I find that odd."

"What are you trying to imply?" asks a defensive and annoyed Darren.

"Why is it that this mysterious man, who could very well be the devil incarnate, treats you like his favoured son?" asks Dave.

"Well, if he's killing us anyway and taking the money back, what difference does it make?" replies Darren.

"But you said Bob probably got punished for getting identified. He could just be tying up a loose end," retorts Dave. "But you still got paid double. And it's not like you had a tough job to do."

"Well, neither did you!" interjects Darren.

"Involved a lot more work than you," Dave replies bluntly.

"Why the antagonism? It makes me sad," replies Darren after calming himself down.

Riley looks up in confusion and begins to piece together something in his mind.

"Well, it fucking makes me dandy!" responds Dave.

Darren strikes the table hard in anger and ends up breaking it. He spills his drink in the process. "I don't know what your problem is, but I don't have to take it," he says. He storms out of their hideout, slamming the door behind him.

"Was it something I said?" barks Dave.

Riley gives Dave a quizzical look, which was a mix of anxiety and wonder. "No, but it's something Darren said."

"I don't' know what your problem is, but I don't' have to take it," Dave says, remembering.

"No! Before that."

Dave ponders for a second. "Why the antagonism?"

Riley also joins him to say the last line. "It makes me sad."

"Have you heard such an unusual phrase before?" Riley asks.

"Yes!"

Riley gets excited.

"Just now," he kills Riley's excitement.

"No, I mean before today."

"No, I haven't."

"But if you heard it before, you'd remember it. Right?"

"Yeah probably," answers Dave.

"My point exactly," Riley says with finality.

"Have you heard it somewhere before?"

"Yes. And I've been trying to remember where, ever since Darren spoke those words. And I finally did."

"Where?" Now, Dave was the one who was excited.

"In a strange room while sitting at a table with a light pointed directly at my face. Said by a man whose face I couldn't get a look at."

Dave and Riley look at each other, and it was clear what they had to do next and where they had to go. But one other thing was even clearer.

"One drink for the road?" Dave asks Riley.

"Yes. A double." answers Riley.

—X—

— CHAPTER 13 —

It's Time

Darren walked down a busy street in a foul mood with a headache that just didn't want to quit. What happened to Bob was still on his mind. He couldn't shake the image off. Revenge was the only thing he wanted. An eye for an eye. A poetic end. He had vivid visions of ripping the perpetrator's arm off and beating him to death with it. Normally, such thoughts would make Darren feel uneasy, but right now it didn't. His anger had consumed all of him.

And what Dave had said really got to him. How dare he question his loyalty? When had he ever given any one of them a chance to doubt him? But he knew deep down inside that Dave was in the same pain as him. He lashed out because he didn't know what to do. He recalled a certain memory from sixth form. He and Dave were interested in the Watson twins. They knew they had one chance with them. Drunk on courage and a six-pack, the pair of them broke into their neighbour, Mr Murray's home, and nicked the keys to his beamer. They drove around with the

Watson Twins for hours before abandoning the car in Shoreditch. Since it was found blemish-free, Mr Murray didn't follow up with the coppers too much. He was just happy he had gotten his car back. That was always a good memory to look back on for Darren. It wasn't long after this that Dave began running with the Tower Hamlets crew. And Darren himself caught the eye of a certain someone after single-handedly robbing a high-end jewellery store in Marble Arch. Many years and a prison sentence later, fate brought them back together, along with Bob and Riley. And since then, they had made many great memories together. A single misunderstanding like this shouldn't tear them apart. This is why it was important for Darren to stay calm and think rationally. Be the bigger person and figure this out. So far he had been the exact opposite. On edge and cranky.

What he really needed was something to eat. A perfect thought to have as we walked in front of a Turkish chicken & chip shop. The delicious aroma of the meat, spices and sauces was enough to make him feel weak in the knees. This was the perfect pick-up he needed. But there were so many delicious choices and so little strength in him to figure it out. He was going to wing this decision. Trust his instinct. Listen to his empty, growling gut. He steps into the restaurant.

A few minutes later, he emerged from within carrying a nice lamb shawarma with him. His instinct had made the right call. He ate it hungrily and messily as he walked down the road. He felt his brain rebooting, the alcohol in his blood dissolving, and his headache receding. He finally had what he wanted most since he woke up: a clear head. And that clear head reminded him of something important. He had dinner tonight with Judy and his mum. They were going to meet for the first time. This was an important day, probably the most important day in his life. It had to go well. This would normally be the time he would begin to feel queasy and uneasy, but he didn't. He felt good. What was happening felt right. The fact that this felt right made him feel even better.

He stopped at a florist to buy 2 bouquets of flowers. "One for Judy and one for Mum, wow I'm a good boyfriend and son." He hummed to himself while purchasing them. The food had done wonders to his mood. He had a little dance in his steps as he walked down the road smiling at passers-by who probably thought he was mental.

He skips past a jewellery shop and stops dead in his tracks. Twirls around to take a look at what was on display. His eyes light up. He runs inside the shop.

Comes out less than a minute later. He knew exactly what he wanted, and he paid for it in cold hard cash. A simple, beautiful gold ring with intricate etchings and a diamond as the centrepiece. "It's time!" he muttered to himself, and he knew he was ready for this. He was sure Judy was the one for several months now. On a cold, cold February evening they went to see the Spurs take on the Red Devils. His team did take a 4-0 trouncing but that didn't matter. Not on that day. What mattered was when he looked into her eyes during the match, something inside him kicked. This woman didn't give a lick about football. She called it soccer. Partly to annoy him. But he knew then and there he couldn't live without that annoyance. Not anymore. He loved her. And today he was going to show her how much. He was going to pop the question tonight in front of his mum. He wanted her to be there. He wanted the two most important people in his life to be with him. He felt a little tingle in his body that he hadn't felt since he was 12 years old and mum got him an SNES and Super Mario World for Christmas. He was happy. He was genuinely happy. Probably the happiest he had ever been. And he liked it. And he wanted to feel this way every day. Forever.

He then stopped dead in his tracks. He also remembered how his mum worked two jobs that holiday to get him those gifts. She didn't buy anything for herself. A gift for him was all that she could afford. She did that just for him. She did everything for him since he lost his dad. Since she lost her husband. Darren realises he should have made her meet Judy sooner. He might have been a decent boyfriend, but he had been a crappy son. The guilt would have sunk him, but he knew he couldn't change the past. He could, however, shape the future. And he vowed that his future would have both Judy and his mum. And they would feel that same tingle he felt inside himself just a few minutes ago. He was going to make sure of it. And they would feel like that each and every day.

But he knew that would only happen if he left his line of work behind. Both his jobs. The illegal one and the crappy one. He had the money now. He could buy a house in the countryside and live the rest of his days with Judy and his mum. In a house with a backyard filled with a few dogs. Maybe start a little bakery that would sell doughnut-shaped pizza slices as the in-house special. This all sounded perfect in his head. Now he just needed to make it happen.

Leaving his life in London behind him seemed easy enough. But he knew he needed to do one thing before leaving. Avenge the death of his friend. "It's time!" He muttered to himself again and knew what he had to do next.

CHAPTER 14

SURPRISE

Riley and Dave were at the corner where they each met Mr Shadow for the first time. The lamp post in front of an alley that overlooked Flaming Nero's Pizza parlour. The often-derided piss-pot establishment sold doughnut-shaped pizza slices and also happened to employ their dear friend Darren. But that's something they didn't know. Only Bob did, and he was no more. Darren thought it was too embarrassing to tell them because that's what the job was. And not to forget the apron he had to wear. Dave and Riley, on the other hand, had a much more acceptable and manly day job in construction. Mostly bricklaying, but at least they didn't have to wear an apron.

"Are you nervous, mate?" asks Riley of Dave.

"A little. You?"

"Yeah, kinda. But I really want to shoot this cunt," says Riley, sounding charged up. "I'm itching to use this gun."

"I feel the same way. But we've got to get proof first. And do you really think Darren could be Mr

Shadow? I didn't get a look at his face but I think I would have recognised my friend."

"I'm not sure what I believe in anymore. Bob is dead. And the place where this asshole met us is the only lead we've got."

Dave agrees. They walk into the alley and make the criss-cross turns they made that night to come across the small door to Mr Shadow's lair.

"We can't break it open. It's still early, and someone might see," Dave tells Riley.

"This is where Darren would have been useful. He would have opened this in a cinch."

"Maybe it's unlocked?" Dave says hopefully.

"What are the odds of that?" Riley retorts.

"It's worth a try," Dave responds. He turns the knob and pushes the door. It easily swings open with a rickety sound.

They both look at each other and take out their guns. They walk down the tiny hallway towards the door of the room where their meetings took place. The place was pitch black. Whatever little light eked in didn't travel much, and all the windows were painted black. The only airflow present was because of a tiny ventilation shaft high up on the wall.

They enter the "meeting" room and Riley flicks the light switch on. Right next to him stood a masked man in all black pointing a gun at him. Dave aims his gun at the masked man.

"Drop it!" Dave tells the masked man.

The masked man takes a closer look at them with the lights on, puts his gun away, and removes his mask. It was Darren. "Surprise!" he says in a half-mocking tone.

Dave lowers his gun. Riley takes a long, deep breath and removes a cigarette from his pocket to light it. Darren also rolls a cigarette for himself.

"What the hell are you guys doing here?" says Darren after a particularly long puff.

"What are **we** doing here? What are **you** doing here? And what's with the mask?" Dave asks angrily.

"So I don't get recognised. I came here to look for clues to find Mr Shadow," retorts Darren.

"That's why we also came," Riley tells Darren. "Did you find anything?"

"No, not really. But I did have a thought. What if Bob was killed by the people we stole from? And they tortured him to get to know about the rest of us?" replies Darren.

"Yes, we thought of that too. That's why we came here. To look for clues. Because we don't know who we fucked over," Dave answers.

"I know who we fucked over. It was in the details in the manila envelope," replies Darren.

"You know who we stole from? Who?" interjects Riley.

"Wait, you didn't get this in the details either? Neither did Bob. Why is that?" asks Darren.

"Why don't you tell us, favoured son?" Dave interrupts rudely.

"Let's not start with this again," Riley stops things from escalating. "Who did we steal from?

"Louie James," answers Darren.

Riley's face dropped the second he heard that name.

"That cupcake fashion designer?" asks a visibly confused Dave.

"He's no cupcake, Dave. He has a lot of cops on his payroll and is a major controller of the cocaine and ecstasy trade in the city. He doesn't look it, but he is one of the most dangerous people in London," answers Riley.

"Are you shitting me?" interjects Dave.

"No, Riley's right. I used to work for Louie. Years ago," says Darren. He immediately recalls the first time he had met Louie. One of Louie's closest associates, Matt Jones, had reached out to him for a meeting. Darren was immediately awed by Louie's presence and aura. Louie, in turn, was impressed by Darren's recent escapades. He had robbed a jewellery store in Marble Arch. Louie had offered him to be a part of his crew then and there. Darren had thought about that proposition deeply, but only for a moment. His gut had told him it was the right thing to do. What followed was years of the "high life" interspersed with a host of illegal activities and some violence.

"Was it a job for him that got you busted?" asks Dave of Darren, snapping him out of his daydream.

"Yes! Some of his product was stolen by a bunch of Pakis. I was sent to get it back. A quick B&E job. But the coppers showed up and caught me with the evidence. I didn't say a word about him to the fuzz. Kept my mouth shut just like I was asked. What did I get in return? Nothing. No bailout. No severance. Nothing. He let me rot in prison and take the fall. After everything I did to serve him."

An uncomfortable silence takes over. Darren looked troubled remembering this part of his life. Dave wanted to comfort him but didn't know where to start. But there were more pressing matters at hand. And Riley understood that better than anyone.

"Okay, so we now know who we fucked over. And let's assume they got to know about Bob through some dirty cops or investigating on their own. They find Bob, take their money back and torture him to find out about us," Riley conveniently sums up their predicament.

"Yeah, that's about right. But we don't know if Bob told them anything," mutters Darren.

"Well, we're still alive so there's your silver lining," says Riley.

"But we can't say for sure that Louie's people did this to Bob?" questions Dave. "This is just like how it is with Mr Shadow. We don't know anything."

"No, no! It's different. We can find out if Louie's people did this or not," interjects a confident-sounding Darren. "And I know just the person who'll tell us everything. Matt Jones. One of Louie's top people. And I just know where to find him. Let's go."

Riley and Dave were in agreement and felt all charged up.

An alarm goes off on Darren's phone. He takes his crappy little burner out to turn it off and then notices the time. "Fuck! fuck! fuck! fuck and a half!"

"What happened, Darren?" asks Riley.

"Boys, I'll join you two in a few hours. I have to go take care of something. Let me get back, then we'll go after Matt." Darren says in an almost rushed and pressured speech.

"What happened? Settle down, mate. You look worried," Dave tells Darren with some degree of concern.

"I'm late! Late for dinner. With Judy and me mum. They're meeting tonight. For the first time." Darren tries to explain.

"Well, fucking cancel it. We've got more important things to do," Dave says bluntly.

Darren didn't take this too kindly. "Nothing is more important than this dinner to me. Nothing!"

The boys look unhappy and unconvinced. Darren knew what he had to do. He moves his hand into his coat pocket as if he's reaching for a gun. Riley and Dave don't know what to expect. They both instinctively go for their guns. Darren takes out the diamond ring from his pocket. The boys understand almost immediately, and the tension drops.

"I know I can be difficult. I'm truly sorry for it. But this is something I must do tonight. Because I've decided I'm going to leave this life behind me. Start a new one with a family. But I can't do that until we take down whoever killed Bob. Whether it's Louie or Mr Shadow or some other cunt."

"Good luck, mate," Dave shakes Darren's hand and pulls him close for a hug. "But I'll be honest. One thing is bothering me."

Darren is taken aback. He tentatively asks. "What is?"

"You're over here ready to marry this girl, and the pair of us have never met her. We're your best mates. We've known each other since we were young'uns." Dave answers.

Riley adds. "We were half sure she's not even real. She is real, right?" He begins to snicker.

Dave joins him for a laugh. Darren knew he deserved this. But he had been adamant about keeping his two worlds apart. It did feel like the right thing to do. But was it still?

Riley continues. "Not making her meet Dave, I can understand. What about me? I've never even been to prison."

Dave interjects. "That's only because we give you the easy jobs to do, pup."

Riley shoves Dave in jest, who just continues to laugh. They begin to fight like siblings.

Darren looks at his two friends bickering and imagines Judy interacting with them. He could only imagine it as a good thing. He smiles. "You fellas are right. Let her say yes, and then we get together and have a few drinks." He still wasn't sure that he wanted his two worlds to collide.

"What if she says no?" Enquires Riley

Darren hadn't thought about that possibility. Also, he didn't want to. "We still get together for drinks."

The three of them share a hearty laugh. The first time they'd done that since last night. Since Bob. But then they remembered Bob, and the laughter ebbed away. That uncomfortable silence returned.

Dave, however, broke it as it was time to get things moving. He turns to Darren. "Good luck mate. I know she'll say yes. But send us the details on Matt. We'll keep him ready for you. It's time we give Matt Jones a little..."

"Surprise!" says Riley loudly while putting a silencer on his gun.

CHAPTER 15

FRENCH FOOD

A black cab stopped in front of a fancy French restaurant in Oxford Circus. The door swung open, and out came Darren dressed in an impeccable black formal jacket with black trousers and a black shirt. He had replaced his black knock-off Nike trainers with shiny leather formal black shoes. He had clearly gone shopping. And not at Primark. It was safe to say that he looked good. Was sure to draw a lot of attention and eyeballs. That is until he put on a black fedora with an eagle feather. Now Darren thought he looked good. He was wrong!

But the universe luckily had other plans. A strong gust of wind blew down Oxford Circus and took Darren's fedora with it. He tried to grasp at it, but it slipped from between his fingers. All he was able to hold on to was the feather, and he ended up mangling it. The fedora landed in the middle of the road, which was wet and dirty from the endless annoying drizzle of London. "It's not that bad," Darren thought to himself and took a step to retrieve it. But before he could step off the sidewalk, a double-decker bus came and ran over the fedora, trying its best to merge it with the tarmac. Darren, at that moment, realised that he might not need the hat. He takes out the bouquets of flowers he bought earlier and lets the black cab go.

He entered the restaurant and was guided by a waiter to his table. He sat himself down comfortably and admired the decor. It was tasteful and elegant. He hoped the food would be just as good. He had never had French food except for crepes and French fries. "How bad could it be?" he thought to himself but knew he had to prepare for the worst. Luckily, there was always McDonald's down the road.

The waiter brings over the wine list, and Darren points at the most expensive one. He had no idea what was good but was always tempted to try the expensive stuff. The wine that snobs and poshos drooled over at their parties with other landed gentry and monocle-wearing, opera-attending, butler-having thespians. He takes a look at the menu and can't understand a thing. It was all written in French. "But this is England! Not France. They shouldn't use their stupid, stuffy, mean-sounding language here," Darren thought, racistly. McDonald's was clearly the better choice in his mind.

"Hello, love." A sweet familiar voice breaks his train of thought. He lowers the menu and sees Judy. She was looking the hottest she had ever looked. Even hotter than the Avril Lavigne concert when she wore jeans and a T-shirt and had her hair tied in a messy bun. Why was that the hottest? Darren wasn't sure. But watching her sing along to the performance was the cutest thing he had ever seen. And it gave him the urge to impregnate her. It was a hard urge to fight, but he did. At this moment, he felt that urge return. Only this time, it was stronger. He wasn't sure if he'd be able to keep it in check. Judy wore a saucy but elegant blue dress. Also, not from Primark. It left little to the imagination. But also, enough. Darren wanted to have her right then and there. And it started to show visually around the crotch area. She moves closer and gives him a peck. That led to things standing up in perfect attention. Darren tries to stand up to greet Judy properly. He uses the menu to cover certain parts of himself. Judy realises what's happening and giggles. "I'm glad I still have this effect on you nearly two years later."

"And you always will," Darren says sweetly.

"Aww, you're such a wuss," she holds his face tightly and gives him a big, long, sloppy kiss. "But that's why I love you."

Darren was overjoyed on hearing this. It made him blush and look all cute and vulnerable. He still had his erection, though. "How was your day?"

"Had a lot more work than I expected on a Saturday. Which is supposed to be none. This client wants an auto loan for an Astra and is just bombarding me with all these questions." Judy sounded exhausted. It had been a long week for her. "Didn't expect you Brits to have the same terrible work culture when I moved here from across the pond. But I guess banks are shit everywhere..."

Darren watched her speak and just smiled. Every time she talked about the mundane aspects of her life, he wanted to hear more. It was the exact thing he wanted in his life. Stillness. Peace. Judy brought that with her. He wanted to be a better person because of her. For her. Just so he could be with her. He knew in the back of his mind that the moment she would learn the absolute truth about him, she'd leave. And she would be right to. But he knew he would do anything to be with her. And with the two million, he could give her the life she wanted. But what if he had to choose between her and the money? Then what?

Judy snaps Darren back from Wonderland. "Alice, don't go down the rabbit hole."

Darren realised he'd just been smiling at her, not listening to a word she said. He did that from time to time. He suddenly remembered he had bought flowers for her and gives her one of the bouquets.

"Fancy restaurant and flowers. What's the special occasion?" asks Judy teasingly.

"I hope it's because you're meeting me," a raspy older female voice interjects in the conversation, grabbing both Darren and Judy's attention. It was Darren's mum. She was dressed in simple and inexpensive clothing, but she carried herself very well. She took a good look at Judy in a disarming way. Judy didn't know why, but she felt a little self-conscious. Suddenly, she wasn't sure if she was dressed appropriately or like some cheap harlot who found herself in an entanglement with her son.

"Mum!" Darren goes and gives his mum a big, long hug. She hugs him back even tighter. They both had missed each other dearly. He hands her the other bouquet. "These are for you. And Judy, this is my mum, Patricia."

Judy was usually a confident lass, but meeting Darren's mum made her feel like a 16-year-old virgin from the industrial age about to be wedded to the Duke's son. Pretty, special, important, the centre of attention but eventually due for a bloody ploughin! "Hello, Patricia. It's so lovely to finally meet you."

"Yes, it's been a long time coming. But I'm sure my wonderful son has done everything in his power to delay this."

Judy realised in an instant that Patricia had a tongue. Plus, Darren knew it was true. He had been delaying this day for over a year. In hindsight, it felt so trivial. But that is why it was important for tonight to be perfect. After all, he had the greatest of surprises.

"Let us not dwell on the past. Let's have a wonderful meal together. And perhaps there might be a surprise at the end." This had both Judy and Patricia intrigued. Now they had expectations. Darren didn't like people having expectations of him. Except in bed, of course, because he was 'awesome at sex and stuff'. "Come, let us all have a seat. Take a look at the menu. Have a little conversation. Look, even the wine is here."

A waiter brings the wine and hands it to Darren. Darren knew exactly what he had to do next. He begins to open the cork with his mouth. "No, sir! Please! Let me handle it." The waiter opens the bottle and pours some wine into each of their glasses. Leaves the bottle in a bucket of ice. Judy was in splits but tried her best not to laugh at Darren's boorish actions.

Patricia started LOL-ing. "You're a chav, Darren. Always have been. Fancy clothes and fine dining aren't going to change that. You have too much of your father in you. And thank God for that. God rest his soul."

Darren didn't have a response for that. Plus, he completely agreed with her. He was a chav, the poster definition of one. But since Judy and his mum were meeting, he thought it was important to dress up well.

Judy bursts out laughing as well. "I agree, Patricia. He's such a chav. He also yells at the telly whenever his team loses."

"He still does that? Well, I guess some things never change. But he's mostly your problem now. So you deal with it." comes Patricia's reply.

They seemed to be getting along well. This was even better than Darren had planned. Sure, they were making fun of him, but that was acceptable. He picks up the menu. "What should we have? The 'Cuisses de Grenouille' (butchers the pronunciation completely) sounds quite exquisite."

"Those are frog legs, love," Judy tells him.

Darren drops the menu in disgust. "What the fuck is wrong with these Frenchies? Who the fuck eats frogs and their fucking legs? Don't they have enough chickens, pigs and cows? That's why I fucking hate the French. And this wine tastes like shit. Why is it so expensive? Even 5 quid Tesco brand is better than this."

"I agree," replies Patricia. "But I'm still gonna chug all of it down."

"Well, of course. Can't let any of it go to waste. Especially if it's expensive," adds Judy.

"Yes, I couldn't agree more with you, petal," Patricia tells Judy. "Darren, I don't mean to cause a damper on your well-planned night of fanciness, but I'm feeling quite peckish and I'd much rather have a Big Mac and some chicken nuggets."

Darren wanted to smile and shout out "yes." But he didn't know how Judy felt.

"Yes, Patricia. That'll be wonderful. I wouldn't mind a cheeseburger and some fries," Judy tells Darren.

Darren looks at Judy and knows he has found the perfect woman for himself. He wants to pop the question now more than ever. But the setting has to be perfect. And it isn't going to be this restaurant. He picks up the wine bottle and pours it out into all 3 of their glasses. "Whoever chugs their glass first gets to choose the happy meal toys."

Once it was decided that Patricia would get to choose the Happy Meal toys, the three of them made the short walk to McDonald's and sat themselves down in a cosy booth not too far away from the cashier. The wine-chugging had its effect on all three of them. It had loosened them up and made them all quite a bit more chatty. Patricia and Judy were thick as thieves, planning a grand shopping day in Camden. Darren encouraged them to have it tomorrow so he could invite Riley over for some FIFA. In reality, they needed to find Mr Shadow and find out if he had killed Bob.

"I'm gonna go stand in the queue to order," Darren tells them while forcing himself up. He stood in the line with a few people ahead of him. This was going to take longer than he wanted it to. Luckily, he was easily distracted by the circular fluorescent lights. They looked like floating halos, and he wanted to jump up to them screaming, "I'm an angel." But he would do no such thing. He promised to Judy and his mum that he'd behave.

His phone starts ringing. He takes it out of his pocket and peeks to see who's calling. It's Riley. He looks at the time and it is still early. He wanted to ignore the call but doesn't. He answers it instead. "Hey Riles. Didn't expect you to call so early. I'm still at dinner."

"Hey, bud. Yeah, I thought so. But listen. Something has come up, and I'm gonna need your help regarding the whole Matt thing. I'm coming to pick you up right now. Where are you?"

Darren could hear traffic in the background. "Look, Riles. Tonight is important for me. I need some more time. Plus, I haven't even… You know! Popped the question."

"Well, stop being a wanker and get it done. I'm calling you because this is an emergency. Now, where are you?"

Darren knew Riley wouldn't call unless it was really that important. "I'm at McDonald's at Oxford Circus. How much time are you reaching in?" His plan to pop the question was going to have to wait.

"Your special dinner is at McDonald's? Are you sure you're not proposing with an onion ring?"

"Call me when you've reached," Darren cuts the call and takes a good long look at Judy and his mum. They were doing fine without him. Probably talking about his dad, he imagined. Maybe he could just sneak out, and they wouldn't even notice? Darren needed an excuse to leave that didn't rouse suspicion. But what could that be?

"Hello. My name is Bob. Can I please take your order?" says the polite cashier to Darren, interrupting his train of thought. Darren was almost annoyed, but then he got an idea. He smiles at the cashier and gives his order.

A few minutes later, he joins Judy and Patricia with two packed trays of food and cola. He hungrily grabs a fistful of French fries and stuffs them in his mouth. "We're still having some French food."

"Don't spit on me, boy," Patricia scolds him while digging in. Judy goes after the fries, pretty much gobbling them up. Darren messily eats his burger, letting the meat's tender juices drip down his chin. They all looked happy.

My perfect little family, Darren thought to himself. This was already one of his favourite memories to look back on. That tingle of happiness was back in his stomach. But he knew Riley was close by. And he would have to leave early. If Darren wanted the perfect little family life, he would have to tie up some loose ends. And soon. Darren knew what he had to do next. He finishes his burger.

"Girls. I'm sorry, but I'm going to have to leave," Darren tells them.

"But why? It's still early. I thought we could head to the cinema," Judy retorts.

"Or head to a pub," adds Patricia.

"I'd love but I got some bad news on the phone," Darren begins to explain. "Judy, remember around lunch I got a call to come to Bob's."

"Yes, I remember. How is he? What happened to him? It completely slipped my mind," Judy answers.

"You mean your friend Bob from, you know?" Patricia inquires. Judy wonders what Patricia meant by 'you know'.

"Yes, Mum. The same Bob. He was mugged last night in Turnpike Lane. Was in a terrible shape. And…" Darren might have been partially lying but he felt every ounce of pain for real. "… I just got word from the hospital." Darren looks at both of them with tears in his eyes. "He didn't make it." Darren starts quietly weeping.

"I'm so sorry, love," Judy holds Darren's hands.

"I'm very sorry to hear this, dear. When did he pass away?" Patricia asks.

"While I was waiting in line to order," Darren answers.

"Why didn't you say something sooner?" Judy asks him.

Darren hadn't thought the lie through. "I didn't want to ruin dinner. Or at least what was left of it." But he was good under pressure. "I'm sorry, but I'll need to leave. Take care of some arrangements."

"Yes, of course, love. Don't worry about us. You need to be there. In fact, I'll come with you. I can't let you deal with it on your own," Judy tells Darren.

"I agree. I'll tag along as well. It breaks my heart. Poor Bob. He was such a nice man," Patricia chimes in.

Darren knew he had to choose his words carefully. "That's very sweet of both of you. But I'll be fine." That was a good start. "Riley and Dave will be there too." Kind of a desperate addition. "And I don't want to ruin the rest of the night for you two. You're both right. It's early. Go to the cinema." That was a good recovery. "Or a nice pub. There's one around the corner that's managed by a nice older single gentleman from the Caribbean, Mum. I think you two would hit it off."

"Caribbean!" Patricia was surprised but jubilant. "Come, Judy. We must go. Drinks are on me. Quickly finish your chips."

Darren's phone starts vibrating. He takes a look and sees it's Riley. "Alright, you two. I'm going to have to head off."

Darren hugs them both and looks to leave.

"It's terrible that you weren't even able to get to your surprise," Patricia tells Darren.

"I completely forgot," Judy adds. "What is it?"

Darren thought about telling them about the ring, but it didn't seem like the right thing to do tonight. Not anymore. However, he was adamant about having that perfect setting again. "We might have been too hard on the French food. It deserves another shot. Pack your bags. We're going to Paris. We leave the day after."

Judy and Patricia begin celebrating and thanking him. But Darren had drowned out all sounds. For him, the only thing in focus was the job at hand.

CHAPTER 16

ALMOST THERE

Darren steps out of McDonald's just as Riley pulls up in Dave's car, an old grey Ford Focus. Darren opens the front passenger seat door and finds the car completely hotboxed, with the stereo blasting some lyrical-less, bass-heavy EDM. Darren hops inside, and Riley pushes the pedal to the metal. Speeding down the road, they barely cross a traffic light as it turns red.

Riley passes the spliff to Darren and takes a good look at him. "You're dressed quite fancy for some McDonald's."

Darren takes a big, long puff and cranks open the window a bit to let the smoke clear out. He then lowers the music volume. "What do you wear to McDonald's? Trainers and a jumper? You fuckin chav! Where's Dave?"

"Home. Setting things up. Loaned me his car. Told me to go get Matt."

"Alone?" asks Darren.

"I told him I could handle it. I could tell he wanted to stay back and clean that damn carpet."

Darren looks disappointed.

"He told me to ask you." Riley answers. "The only thing is I knew tonight was important for you. So I figured I'd go solo. Give you some time with your girl and mum."

"Thanks, Riles. But I'm glad you called me instead of going solo. Matt Jones is a very dangerous man. A crazy, unhinged personality who enjoys being in pain as much as he likes inflicting it" Darren tells Riley. "So, do you know where he is?"

Darren feels a sharp stab on his right bicep and he screams. He turns around to see Matt Jones still gagged and mostly tied up. Matt had been able to loosen one of his hands and had stabbed Darren, not too deeply, with the corkscrew of a Swiss Army knife.

"Fucking hell, you're loose again!" Riley screams. He puts the spliff behind his ear and takes out a metal pipe from under his seat. "Darren! Take hold of the wheel!"

Darren was still in shock from the stabbing. He nods and grabs hold of the steering wheel with his bleeding arm. Riley takes off his seatbelt, pushes his seat as far back as possible with his foot still on the accelerator, turns around, and starts whacking Matt with the metal pipe. "Why don't you stay down, you sneaky cunt?" Matt fights back with punches of his own.

Darren does his best to keep the car in its lane. What was coming next, however, was not going to be easy to deal with. A frail old lady was crossing the road just as the light turned red for them. Darren blows the horn frantically. The old lady doesn't hear it. "Deaf cunt!" he thought to himself but shouted out, "Brake Riley! Brake!" frantically.

"I'm doing just that." Riley tells Darren while repeatedly trying to break Matt's ribs into a million little pieces with his metal pipe.

The car was in striking distance from the frail old woman now. She still hadn't noticed them. Darren turns the steering wheel ever so slightly and pulls on the handbrake about halfway. They slow down just enough for Darren to manoeuvre the car and narrowly miss the old woman who even now hadn't noticed them. Darren turns around to make sure she's alright, but when he looks back ahead, there were bigger challenges.

They were approaching a suburban intersection with a lot of pedestrians and cyclists. Some of them were children. Darren grabs hold of Riley by his trousers and hoists him towards the backseat, invariably helping Riley apply more weight on Matt and choke him down with the metal pipe.

"Yes, Darren! Good! Push me harder from the back! Aaaah! Go harder!"

"Stop making it sound sexual," Darren retorts.

"Don't stop what you're doing! I'm so close to the end! Push me harder, please!" Riley keeps telling Darren, who lifts him up and throws him completely on top of Matt using almost all his strength. Riley holds Matt down with his weight, takes the spliff from behind his ear, and puts it in his mouth. "Pass me the lighter, Darren?"

Darren was finally able to get in the driver's seat and take control of the car mere moments before it was going to crash into a lamppost. He brakes hard and swerves the car back on the road but was unable to stop it bouncing over a speed bump.

The bump sent Riley up in the air long enough for Matt to get his hand loose properly and choke Riley. Matt had a death grip around his neck and wasn't going to let go of it. Riley tried his best to call Darren for help, but all he could manage was a soft whimper that nobody could hear. He still somehow had the spliff in his mouth though.

Darren finally brings the car to an acceptable speed on a somewhat tranquil road and breathes a sigh of relief. He finds the lighter in the cupholder and holds it back for Riley. "Here's the lighter, Riles. Take a few quick puffs and pass it along like a good lad," Darren dangles the lighter but Riley wasn't taking it. He peeks in the rearview mirror and sees Riley with the spliff in his mouth but wasn't able to see that he was getting choked to death. "Riley! Riley! The lighter."

Riley tries to speak, but he's super low on oxygen now. His arms had gone all dangly, and he felt too weak to fight back. He decides to try hitting Matt one last time, a Hail Mary punch. He musters all the strength he has and pulls his arm back for a punch but ends up hitting Darren on the back of the head with his elbow.

"You fucking prick!" Darren yells and momentarily loses control of the car.

It goes haywire enough for Matt to go off balance and loosen his grip on Riley. Not wanting to waste time, Riley quickly takes aim and punches the living daylights out of Matt. He takes in a big breath of oxygen and notices the lighter that Darren still had dangling about. "Cheers, mate." Riley lights the spliff and takes a long victory puff. Blows it out on Matt and burns his face a bit with the lighter. The still gagged Matt squirms in pain. Riley's phone begins to ring. He punches Matt again, knocking him out cold. Takes out his phone and sees it's Dave. He passes the spliff to Darren and answers the phone. "Yes, Dave."

"Where are you guys?" asks Dave.

"Almost there!" answers Riley and cuts the phone.

CHAPTER 17

Don't Ruin the Carpet

Darren and Riley reach Dave's old, dilapidated block of flats and luckily find a parking spot right outside. Now they just needed to figure out how they were going to sneak an unconscious Matt up to the 5th-floor flat.

"I have an idea, Darren, on what we should do," says Riley.

"So do I except my idea is perfect. So we're going to do that instead," interjects Darren.

"But my idea is perfect too."

"But there's only one perfect idea. If you say your idea is perfect then it has to be the same as my idea because I know my idea is perfect," Darren replies confidently.

"Makes perfect sense. Alright, so we tell each other our idea on 3?"

"Agreed! One... Two... Three!"

"Weekend at Bernie's." They speak out in a chorus together. It felt like a perfect moment for them to share a smile.

A few minutes later, they walk inside and into a musty-smelling, run-down hallway, holding an unconscious Matt upright and dragging him along. Riley wanted to tie his feet with theirs, but Darren argued that they could just say their mate had had too much to drink. It was a much more elegant solution than perfectly imitating an '80s comedy film. Riley had agreed to disagree but realised there was no rope in the car. He did manage to convince Darren to put a pair of sunglasses and a hat on Matt. Darren agreed to it so they could cover his black eye and the bleeding cuts on his head. They reach the lift and come to a crushing realisation: it was out of order, and they'd have to take the stairs. For 5 whole floors!

They had carried Matt 2 floors up when they really began to feel his weight. "He's put on more than a few stones since I worked with him," remarks Darren.

"Tell me something, mate. What does he do for Louie James?" asks a curious Riley.

"Basically anything. Drives Louie around. Will even fetch his groceries if asked nicely enough. Controls most of the trade for him on the west side from Acton to Drayton. And hires people like me to do their dirty work. Long story short; he's one of the few people who knows everything Louie does." Darren wipes the sweat off his forehead. "Come on, Riles. We're on the final stretch. Let's give it our all. Dave is waiting for us."

Riley agrees and puts more effort in.

"Where did you find him?" Darren asks inquisitively.

"Coming out of an off-licence. Smacked him on the head with a metal pipe. Didn't go down straight away, this one. He's a fighter."

"Oh, you haven't seen anything yet," says Darren, thinking it added drama.

A few difficult minutes later, they reached Dave's floor and his hallway. They waited for the coast to be clear and brought him to Dave's doorstep. Darren sharply knocked on the door. They could hear footsteps hurrying towards the door. The latch was opened, and Dave slowly opened the door to see his companions. "You're late."

"The lift isn't working," Darren answers.

The three of them tie Matt up on a chair in the bedroom. Dave had covered the floor and walls in plastic sheets. Darren asked him if he intended to cut Matt up into little pieces like some psychopath?

Dave yelled at him and said he didn't want his carpet ruined. He had just had it cleaned. Riley had some great jokes about Dave being a serial killer but was paranoid that it might be true. The "kill-room" was just purely unsettling and could give Dexter some competition.

Darren slaps Matt to wake him up. He gets up and looks around, all bug-eyed, waiting for everything to come into focus. Once it does, he takes a good, long look at his captors.

"Well, well, well, if it isn't Darren Turner. It's been a long, long time. And who are these two cunts? The balls to your prick?" Matt spoke in his thick cockney accent with his usual charm.

Darren punches Matt hard on the jaw. "We're the ones who are going to be asking the fucking questions."

Matt spits out some blood on the floor and looks at Darren with pure hatred. He wants to break free and fight back.

Dave pokes Darren to get his attention. "Imagine that blood on my carpet. It would never come off."

Darren looks at Dave incredulously and turns back to face Matt. "Now where were we?"

"You were supposed to ask me questions before you decided to eye-fuck your fat little boy toy," Matt says without a care in the world. He had been tortured way too many times beyond caring.

"We know you guys got to Bob. How did you get to know about him? And how did you find him?" asks Darren.

"What the fuck are you talking about? And who the fuck is Bob?" Matt looked just as puzzled as the rest. "Why am I here?"

Darren felt his fists clenching. His blood boiling. The anger in him rising. But he had to stay calm for now. For Bob. "Let me help clarify things. How is Louie doing?"

"Not the best, to be honest. There was an incident last night," answers Matt.

"Oh, you don't say. Does it involve a sultan's bed, the lover's nest, a golden key, no house to sleep, and 5 million pounds less?" Darren was quite proud of his on-the-spot limerick. So were Dave and Riley. Who was he kidding? Darren had been working on that limerick for hours, making notes on his phone.

"It was you guys! Oh, you guys have no fucking idea how much trouble you're in. Louie is going to take his time torturing you cunts," Matt spits out angrily. He calms himself down a bit and lets out a devious smile. "You could give back his money to me right now. I'll make sure he lets you all live." He licks his own swollen, bloody lips.

"If we hand you the money, you'll kill us without hesitation. I don't trust you. I did once and…" Darren stops himself and becomes melancholic for a moment.

Dave and Riley look at each other. They had guessed it.

Darren laughs off his pain and takes out his pistol with a silencer. He points it directly at Matt's temple. "How did you find out about Bob? TELL US NOW!"

Matt spits on Darren's face, who clearly wasn't pleased. He wipes it off himself quietly. There was a discernible amount of tension. Dave felt it. So did Riley.

But Matt didn't. "Fuck you, prick. I'm glad I left you high and dry all those years earlier. For the fuzz to take you away. We knew you couldn't give the Bobbys any usable information. So I asked the big guy if we could cut you loose. And he said yes. Straight away. Didn't have to convince him at all. Because he knew the simple truth. You were a useless cunt…"

Before Matt could finish the sentence, Darren leapt on him and started beating his face to a pulp with the pistol. He then pointed it at his kneecap and shot him without warning. Matt yelled out in pain.

"OH, YOU FUCKING CUNT!" They thought it was Matt, but the sound came from outside.

"It's alright, mates. That's just my neighbour. All he does is watch football on the telly and yell when things go wrong."

Matt was still screaming in pain. Darren punched him square on the jaw and jammed a rag in his mouth to shut him up.

"Calm down, mate," Riley tries to reason with Darren. But he wasn't having it. Darren looks at him and Dave and gestures for them to stay quiet. They both meekly nod and look away.

Darren turns his attention back to Matt. Walks around behind him. Grabs him by his hair and pulls him back. Looks him in the eye with pure distilled hatred. "How did you find out about Bob?"

Matt tries to answer, but he's gagged. Darren pulls out the gag, and Matt starts to cough and catch his breath. "I'll tell you what I know. We got a call in the morning around 7. A deep masculine voice told us where we could find some of our money. He told us to hurry up if we wanted to avoid the fuzz."

"How did this voice sound?" asks Riley cautiously.

"I don't know. It was kind of smooth. But masculine. Heavy like he was a cigar smoker," describes Matt.

"Did he have a subtle softness in his voice?" Dave asks Matt.

Matt thinks about it. "Yeah, I guess."

Darren wasn't convinced by the answer.

"It sounds like Mr Shadow. He tipped them off about Bob," says Riley. Dave nods in agreement.

"Who the fuck is Mr Shadow?" asks Matt.

"So you reached Bob's, killed him and took the money." Darren moves his gun to smack Matt again.

"No! We didn't. I promise! We didn't kill him!" Matt tells them. "I swear to God I'm not fucking lying."

"I don't believe you," responds Darren.

"I don't care if you do. We got that call to come collect some of our stolen money. Our people went to check it out. They saw some cunt dead, tortured, and maimed. We found the money and took it. That's that. End of story."

Dave and Riley were convinced by Matt's story. Darren, not so much. He smiles devilishly at Matt, and it unsettles him a bit.

"You were always good at telling stories," Darren responds. "But if, like me, you hear enough of them, you know they're full of shit just like you."

Matt looks up in anger. "Well, fuck you then, Darren. I can't wait for Louie to find you cunts so you end up dead just like your fucking friend…"

Darren shoots Matt in the temple mid-sentence. The bullet doesn't come out the other end, and there is very little blood splatter from it. It was a clean, professional hit. Dave and Riley are in utter shock, with their mouths left gaping open.

Darren puts his gun away and turns to them. "Get rid of the body at night. I suggest heading out of London and tossing it somewhere in the Thames."

He walks to the door to leave but stops just before exiting. Turns back to them. "Tomorrow we find out who killed Bob. I suggest you grow eyes in the back of your head." Darren leaves, shutting the door behind him. There was no doubt now that with Bob gone, Darren was firmly in charge. Dave and Riley were still in shock. They take another look at Matt.

"Well, at least there's no blood on my carpet," says Dave as Riley looks at him in disbelief.

CHAPTER 18

SOMETHING DOESN'T ADD UP

Riley checks the time on his Shrek watch. Shrek's longer right hand was at 12, and his shorter left hand was at 10. They still had a few hours before they could get rid of Matt's decaying corpse. They spent the last hour wrapping his body up neatly. Well, mostly Riley had. Dave was busy scrubbing the floor and walls of any signs of blood. He was happy his expensive rug, which he stole some years ago, was spotless. "It's a handwoven piece from Kashmir. It'll grow in value," he had always said to them, much to the gang's chagrin. Dave, who was otherwise calm and collected, turned into an absolute nightmare whenever this Kashmiri carpet was involved. The gang did their best to keep as much distance as possible from the carpet, especially Darren, who was a messy eater.

"I think we should call for dinner. We have a long night ahead," Dave says to Riley, who doesn't respond. Riley was lost in Neverland with his thoughts.

"Oye Peter Pan! Fancy some Wendy's?" asks Dave, finally getting Riley to snap out of it.

He looks at Dave, confused about what's asked of him.

"Ground control to Major Tom? Can you hear me, Major Tom?" Dave was as worried as he was annoyed. He was also absolutely famished.

"Something doesn't add up," speaks out Riley finally.

"What doesn't?"

"All of it. Matt's story for one."

"Do you think they killed Bob? But why lie about it?"

"I don't know. Maybe he's telling the truth but... But something's off about all of this. Something just doesn't add up. I feel it deep in my gut. It all just feels uneasy." Riley overuses hand gestures, hoping it conveyed the gravity of the situation.

"Maybe you just need to take a poo." Dave says with a straight face.

Riley is flabbergasted at Dave's reaction. But what bothered him more was that Dave wasn't wrong. Riley really did need to take a poo. He had had a heavy brunch and smoked half a pack of Pall Mall's since then. The double espresso before kidnapping Matt didn't help either. He nods begrudgingly in acceptance. "I do. I do need to poo but… But…"

"Haha, you said butt."

"Shut the fuck up, Dave! I'm trying to be serious here," Riley calms himself down. "As I was saying, something's off. And we need to know what it is." This whole predicament had Riley all riled up. It was clearly bothering him.

Dave finally understands and empathises with Riley. "Go take a shit. Right now it's stuck up your arse and your head. You need clarity in both of those places."

"You're right. And Wendy's does sound nice. I'll have the kids' meal, a Baconator and some chips. You can hold the cola. That shit's fucking nasty and will kill you," Riley says all this while lighting himself another cigarette. He takes a few puffs and holds onto his gut, which was now begging him to run to the John or fetch a fresh pair of pants. "I'll just go make some space for dinner. The train is ready to leave the station." Riley rushes to the facilities.

Dave chuckles and places the food order.

Riley returns 10 minutes later with a clear stomach and a clearer mind. "I've got it!"

"You got what?"

"The part of all of this that doesn't make sense."

"What do you think it is?"

"I'm not completely sure. But I do know what we need to do next. We've got to search Mr Shadow's lair once we're done getting rid of our friend here," Riley points at Matt's wrapped corpse.

"What's the point? We already did. We found nothing."

"No! No, we didn't search it. Darren did. We just took his word for it."

"You think he's lying?" Dave isn't sure.

"He's hiding something for sure. He knew we fucked over Louie James. It was in the job details he was given. We weren't given those details. Why the fuck not? He used to work for Louie who got him arrested, so he's got a motive to get back at him. And most importantly, and I cannot emphasise this enough, he got paid double. Why the fuck did he get paid double?" says Riley emphatically with enthusiastic hand gestures like a mime artist.

Darren getting paid double was on their minds. It was inherently unfair. They all deserved to be paid equally.

Dave thinks about what Riley said. It was all making sense to him. He too now felt that something was off. "You're right. Something's amiss."

"I know. I felt that way since Darren said those words. 'Why the antagonism? It makes me sad.' What an odd fucking thing to say. Mr Shadow said the same thing to me. It's been eating away at me ever since. I've just been trying to make sense of it all." Riley keeps pacing around the room trying to fight his restlessness.

"But do you really think Darren is Mr Shadow? I know you had that inkling earlier today as well," Dave is confused. He continues without letting Riley answer. "I mean they're both tall and lean. We haven't seen Mr Shadow's face. They both love smoking and drinking. Even Bob thought he saw Mr Shadow in the lift." Dave's mind was now racing with a million thoughts. "Oh my God, what the fuck is happening?"

"I don't know if they're the same person or not. But I'm sure they're in it together. And they know a bunch of things we fucking don't." Riley stops pacing and sits himself comfortably on Dave's bed. "I need to eat something or else I'll drive myself crazy."

"I'm starving too. Wendy's should be here any minute. Let's eat, take turns sleeping a few hours. Give this cunt his final rites and get to the bottom of this mystery before he reaches the Atlantic Ocean. How does that sound, Riles?"

"Almost perfect. But I could use a drink or two," Riley smiles.

Dave smiles back and nods in agreement. "I'll go get the whisky."

The doorbell rings. It was Wendy's.

CHAPTER 19

It's the Number of That Pizza Place

Dave and Riley find a secluded spot along the Thames and send Matt to swim with the fishes. His corpse makes a loud splash that no one else hears other than them. It is the middle of the night in the middle of nowhere. They had driven about an hour outside of London towards Reading to find this place among the trees and greens. They weren't taking any chances. Disposing of Matt was the subplot for the day. Now they can focus on what is really important: finding Mr Shadow and learning if Darren and he were in cahoots.

They were determined to get the answers to the questions they had. The questions encircled their minds over and over again like a vulture does to its prey. They sat in pin-drop silence on the drive back to London. The A4 was mostly empty at this hour. They didn't even play any music. The sound of silence was all-consuming and deafening them. Moreover, Dave only had his adult contemporary CDs, and the gang still believed he liked Metallica.

Riley peers out ominously, smoking a cigarette. He offers one to Dave, who refuses. Both of them had no idea what the day had in store for them. But they knew it would lead them somewhere. At least they hoped. They were fuelled with a determination they never thought they had. They were worried for their lives and the money they had chanced upon. They wanted to live, but most importantly, they wanted to live as rich men. They weren't going to give up on the money so easily. They'd give their lives for it and just as easily take someone else's. They just hoped it didn't come to either of this.

Dave drove well within the speed limit. He didn't want to draw any attention. They had waited for the dead of the night to bring Matt's corpse down. The lift was still out of order so they climbed down 5 flights of stairs with his lumbering mass. They saw the coast was clear before loading him into the trunk. They drove through smaller streets and back alleys to get out of London and avoided any and all places where the fuzz could have a checkpoint for drunk drivers and other hooligans prowling out in the night.

Before leaving, they both showered and dressed in their most "pleb" clothes. With a couple of hours of sleep each, they were as well-rested as they could be. And they did take Darren's advice. They grew eyes in the back of their heads. They had a target on them. Louie wanted his money back and killing them was a small price to pay for it. Then there was Mr Shadow. Possibly the reason Bob was dead. His words echoed in their minds. "I'll kill you in the most unimaginable way imaginable." And that's what Bob went through. And there was also Darren. Was he Mr Shadow or just his lackey? It didn't matter. The only thing clear was that he could no longer be trusted. The only thing they were sure of was that they were backed into a corner and they could only trust each other. And they had 2 choices ahead of them. Go on a hunt or get hunted. Fight or flight. Nothing in the middle. No other choices. And they had chosen to fight.

It was almost daybreak when they crossed Flaming Nero's and parked a few streets away.

"I could sure go for a doughnut-shaped pizza right about now," remarks Riley as they cross Flaming Nero's.

"I want a pizza, a doughnut and a doughnut-shaped pizza," replies Dave.

"I promise I'll get you one of each once we're done searching Mr Shadow's lair."

"Sounds good to me," Dave happily began picturing the food he would soon get to devour. He imagined himself encircling his food over and over again like a vulture does to its prey. Wait! I already used that metaphor.

They make their way down the winding alleys and come upon Mr Shadow's lair. A million thoughts rush through their minds on what awaits them on the other side of the door. And all of them are bleak. But there is no turning back.

Riley tries to open the door but it was locked shut. They take a closer look to see if they could open it. They couldn't. Breaking and entering was Darren's speciality. Riley joked about how he could be on the other side of the door like last time.

Dave was, however, in no mood to joke. Or to be discreet. He takes out his gun and kicks the door repeatedly with all his might. A few stern kicks and the door swung open with a rickety sound. They rushed inside and shut the door before drawing any more attention to themselves.

They walk down the hallway and into the room where Mr Shadow had met and given them the details of their jobs. It was just as they remembered it. They recalled their meeting with him as if it were yesterday. The harsh light blasted on their faces. The constant cigar smoke. The top-shelf whisky. And the shadowy figure who sat right in front of them. The enigma who planned the perfect crime. Which they executed nearly perfectly. It would have been perfect if not for Bob. But he paid the price for it. The price they didn't want to pay.

They search through the cabinets and drawers and come across dozens of files. It had everything. All the planning details for the crimes they had committed. There was months of elaborate research. Mr Shadow had taken his time to plan this against Louie James.

"All this planning. It has to be revenge for something," remarks Dave.

"Yeah! No one would go through this much effort otherwise."

"It's making more sense that Darren was in on it from the beginning."

"At least longer than we were."

Dave nods and they get busy going through all the evidence the fuzz and Louie would have loved to have in their investigations.

Dave soon stumbles across their files. All 4 files had detailed information about them down to the minutest of things. They had medical records, sixth form mark sheets, employment records, council tax records, everything you could possibly imagine. Mr Shadow was a perfectionist for sure. And with their gang, Mr Shadow knew he had found the perfect people to execute his plans. They were perfect because they were expendable. "Take a look at these, Riles."

Riley peruses through the files and smiles. "So this is who we are to the rest of the world?"

"There's a file on Darren as well. I'm guessing we could rule him out as being Mr Shadow at least."

"Or maybe the file is here to make us or whoever else believe just that… Either way, he's a person of interest."

That Dave agreed with. "It's easily going to take us a couple of hours to go through everything."

"You're right. Are you already feeling peckish?"

"Since before we got here. But we need to finish this first. Food can wait."

"You're right! I just hope we find the answers to the questions we have."

"If this place doesn't have them, then we've got nowhere else to go. We have to keep searching and hoping."

The pair of them buckled down and studied the files with more effort than they had ever put in sixth form. The threat of death was the world's best motivator. They studied those files with the same intensity as a vulture encircling its…

A couple of hours later, Dave chances upon something peculiar. "Riles! I think I might have found something."

"What is it?"

"This phone number has shown up again and again in different files. I cross-checked it just to make sure. But there are at least 5 instances of Mr Shadow mentioning that he called this number during the last week of planning. Whatever it is, it's the best clue we've gotten so far. It's the only thing I've seen showing up again and again."

Riley takes the different files from Dave and cross-checks the phone number. He is just as convinced as Dave, but only because they didn't have any other clues. "You're right. Let's make a call and see who it is." He takes out his cellphone to make the call.

Dave grabs Riley's cellphone and tosses it away. "STOP! Not from your phone."

Riley realises what he was about to do and takes a deep breath of relief. He also realises that Dave had chucked his phone away and the relief disappeared. "You didn't have to throw my phone away."

"Sorry! That was just the adrenaline." Dave tries to calm himself down. He also takes a few deep breaths.

Riley picks up his phone, sees it's unblemished and pockets it. "I'm glad it's alright. I still have a couple of months left on my contract." He takes out a cigarette and lights it. He needed a moment to himself. To gain some clarity.

"I could use one too," Dave needed that moment too. Riley hands him a fag.

They head outside and walk to the nearest phone booth, which was a few streets away. It was now

10 in the morning. Morning rush was at its peak. They had spent hours searching for clues in the darkness of Mr Shadow's lair. Outside, the sun was shining brighter than it had for the last few days. The warm sunshine felt good on their skin. They hoped it was a sign from God that things would start clearing up for them, just like the sky had. Hope was all they had to cling to. And it would have to do. They hoped that the clue they had found would lead them somewhere. Because without it, they had gotten nowhere.

Dave uses the payphone to make the call. It rings, but no one answers. He and Riley wait for a few minutes and then call again. There is still no answer. Both of them were running thin on patience and were in dire need of nourishment. But this was more important. So they tightened their belts for a little while longer.

"Keep trying. This is all we have," says Riley.

Dave waits another couple of minutes to make the call. Keeps his fingers crossed and hopes the third time was the charm. It was. The phone is answered after a few rings.

"Hello! You've just called Flaming Nero's Pizza. What would you like to order?" comes the voice from the other side.

Dave hangs up almost immediately.

"What happened?" enquires a puzzled Riley.

"It's the number of that pizza place with the doughnut-shaped pizzas. Flaming Nero's," answers Dave as he hangs up the phone.

CHAPTER 20

HONESTY AND A PROPOSAL

Darren wakes up with a hangover and a half. It takes a moment for everything to come into focus. He grabs hold of a bottle of water next to him and gulps it down greedily. He lies there on his bed thinking about the agenda for the day. He and the boys needed to find out who killed Bob. And with Louie being tipped off by Mr Shadow, there was an added layer of concern. Louie would stop at nothing to get his money back from them. Louie would also believe that his lover and assistant were killed by them. This was all too much to take in first thing in the morning. All he wanted to do was take a poo.

The bathroom door swings open, and out walks Judy. She had spent the night following her bar escapade with Patricia. She was prancing around in his t-shirt, which fit her like an oversized. She was going through some of her mail, which she got along with her.

Darren's gaze followed her around his flat. He couldn't believe how lucky he had gotten in life.

He got to be with her. He knew he didn't deserve her. He knew even more that he didn't want to lose her. And now he had the money to give her the life she deserved. And a ring to make it official. He wanted to pop the question. He wanted to do it now. It couldn't possibly wait a moment longer. Sooner or later, his two worlds would collide. It was best to get ahead. He reached for the ring, which was in his side table drawer.

"I just threw up again, love. I need to stop drinking for a bit. Or at least not have as much," remarks Judy.

Darren stops reaching for the ring. It could wait a moment longer. But just a moment more. "Yes, love. I think I should do the same. My head is killing me." Darren had a splitting headache. He got back home after dealing with Matt and proceeded to drink a six-pack of beer while poring over some files he had swiped from Mr Shadow's lair. They didn't reveal anything usable, but the beer did what it was meant to. The first time he killed someone, he was haunted by nightmares for weeks. This time around he felt almost nothing. It felt natural. He drank those beers to help himself sleep and help they did. He was barely able to wake up later at night when

Judy arrived drunk and horny, wanting him. He did the best he could in the circumstances but left a lot to be desired.

"Have all of Bob's funeral arrangements been handled? Did any of his family show up?" asks Judy curiously.

"Sadly, no. They've been estranged for many years now. The funeral will be held once the coppers are done with their investigation."

"Investigation? Did they find something odd about the mugging?"

"Who knows? They're still on the lookout for the mugger," Darren obviously lied. He couldn't tell her what actually happened to Bob. That image was seared inside his head. His hand was severed right off. Whoever killed Bob meant business. And they would do the same to him and the boys. This filled him with a rage he never knew he had. So much so that killing Matt didn't make him feel a goddamn thing. In fact, it made him feel good. That's what he wanted to do with all the others after him and the gang.

But who did kill Bob? That was still a mystery. In his mind, it was Mr Shadow. They needed to get to him before he got to them. But in the back of his mind, there was always Plan B. Fly the coop. Leave London tonight with Judy and his mum. Get away from it all. Let things cool off. But was that even an option? Would Mr Shadow or Louie get to him either way?

"It'd be a shame if no one from his family shows up. Do you know why they were estranged?" asks Judy.

Darren wanted to marry Judy. The first step to a healthy relationship and marriage was honesty. He wanted to tell her the truth about everything. Not just about Bob and his family. But he couldn't just tell her everything all at once. But he also had to start somewhere. He takes a deep breath. "It's because Bob was in prison for 10 years."

Judy is shocked to hear the news.

Darren continues, "For battery and attempted murder. But I know for a fact that it was in self-defence. He just had a shit lawyer."

Judy sits down on the bed next to him. "But you spoke so highly of him. And when I did meet him once briefly, he didn't seem the type. I would never imagine… No! I don't believe it." Judy looks Darren in his eyes deeply with tears. "Is all of this true?"

Darren nods. Judy's face slumps. "Judy!" She looks up at him with teary eyes. "I haven't been completely honest with you either." Darren had no idea where he was going with this. But he knew it was the right thing to do.

Judy is now concerned. "About what?"

"A lot of things. And it's time I came clean." He holds Judy's hand tightly to reassure her. But it didn't assuage her fears. "I met Bob in prison. I was in for 2 years."

Judy's face drops with disappointment and then anger.

Darren continues. "For breaking and entering. I was working this job and the coppers..."

Judy pulls her hand away from Darren. He lets go of it but hopes she'd hold it back. But she didn't. Instead, she hits him. Not once, not twice, but thrice.

"How could you lie to me? After everything we've been through. When did you get out? How?"

Darren cowers in embarrassment. "I got out a few months before we met. That's why I work at Flaming Nero's. No one else was willing to hire me. The owner has a rap sheet of his own so..."

Judy listens patiently. But she doesn't know what to make of it.

He continues, "When I met you, I felt like this missing piece of my life was found. You're the best thing that has ever happened to me. I knew it almost instantly, and I had to turn my life around. And that's all I've tried to do."

Judy is still clearly very angry and rightfully so. This was the ultimate betrayal. The landline starts to ring. It breaks some of the tension. Darren ignores it.

"Aren't you going to answer it?" asks Judy.

"No! It's not important. This moment is. This conversation is."

Judy gets up in anger and starts pacing around. "I can't believe I'm dating a criminal. How could you be so fucking stupid, Judy?" She hits herself on the head repeatedly. "You stupid, stupid girl. Always falling for the wrong kind of boy. I can't believe my mom was right about me. Look at me now! In love with a fucking delinquent."

Darren watches Judy in panic self-destruct mode and thinks to himself that maybe that was too much honesty too soon. But then he has an even crazier thought. The problem with this thought was that it made way too much sense to him in the moment. And Darren was all about the heat of the moment. He ran on pure instinct and what his gut told him to do. And his gut kept repeating the same thing over and over again. "Plan B! Everything else will fall into place." He reaches for the ring away from Judy's gaze and puts it in his shorts pocket. Gets up and goes to calm her down. "Judy, please listen to me once." He tries to hold her still, but she shoves him away.

"NO! Don't you dare touch me. I'm way too mad at you. How could you fucking lie to me about this? And for almost two years. What else are you hiding? Is there another girl? Did I actually meet your mum yesterday?" She keeps pacing up and down the room. "I can't even bear to look at you. I want to just... Just... Just fucking hit you."

"I deserve that."

The phone finally stops ringing.

She stops in her tracks. Turns and goes to Darren. "You're right! You do!" She slaps him on his face repeatedly.

He tries his best to block her hands. She adapts and hits him on other parts of his body. He does his best to keep up, and this frustrates her even more. She kicks him in the groin, and he falls down in pain.

"Does it hurt?" asks Judy sarcastically.

"Yes. A lot," Darren struggles to speak the words out as he rolls over into a foetal position.

Judy towers over him. "GOOD! Now take that pain, multiply it by a million. That's how much your betrayal hurts."

Darren winces in pain and speaks slowly. "I'm sorry. I really am. I know I fucked up. But I didn't want to lose you. I carried this guilt with me all this time."

The landline starts ringing again.

"Oh for fuck's sake!" he exclaims. He pushes himself up onto his knees. "Judy, I'm truly very sorry. But there is one more thing I did lie about."

Judy walks up to him. The phone is still ringing. "What else did you lie about?" She eyes him menacingly.

Darren is frightened. More than he has ever been before. This is how much she meant to him.

"Out with it!!" Judy orders him.

"Yesterday wasn't just about you meeting my mum. There was one other thing I wanted to do before I had to leave."

"What was that?"

He takes a deep breath. "I love you from the bottom of my heart. You really are the best thing that's happened to me. I lied because I was scared to lose you. And I don't want to. At all. I want us to be together forever."

The phone finally stops ringing.

Judy rolls her eyes. All of this sounded like bullshit to her. The same thing she had heard over and over again from other men. And she realised Darren was just like them.

Darren reaches for the ring box inside his pocket and takes it out. It takes Judy a moment to realise what's happening. She is still half in disbelief. Darren opens the box to reveal the ring. She can't believe this is actually happening. Her anger slowly begins to dissipate, and she has an almost half-smile on her face, which she tries her best to hide.

"Will you marry me?" Darren asks confidently and earnestly. "Will you make me the luckiest man in the world?"

Judy doesn't know what to say. She was still angry but also touched. She touches his face softly and with affection. She eyes the ring. It was beautiful. A solid gold ring with some intricate etching and a diamond as the centrepiece. It had a classic timeless design. She loved it. But most importantly, she still loved Darren. She loved him deeply. Even after his lies. But she also remembered his lies. She slaps him hard. Darren holds onto his jaw. She holds his face up to have him look her in the eye. His eyes were full of love, tears, and guilt. She moves close to him and slowly kisses him. And then lets go. His lips were still puckered from the kiss, and he just stood there confused about what was happening.

"Yes! Yes! A million times yes!" Judy screeches out in excitement.

Darren breathes a deep sigh of relief and stands up. Takes the ring out of the box and puts it on her ring finger. Pulls her to him and kisses her passionately. It was the perfect moment that he wished would last forever. His happiness and ecstasy knew no bounds. This was now a core memory. Something he would remember fondly for the rest of his life. Something he would tell his kids and grandkids about. Nothing could ruin this moment for him. It was nothing short of divine… And then the landline started ringing again.

"OH MY FUCKING GOD!" yells Darren at the top of his voice.

Judy giggles. Darren goes to the landline. Picks it up and answers in a monotone. "Hello! You've just called Flaming Nero's Pizza. What would you like to order?" The phone is hung up immediately on the other end.

"Well, that's that." He slams the receiver down.

Judy finds it amusing. "Why did you say that?"

"I don't know. I just didn't want to speak to anyone right now," he holds Judy close to him again. "In this moment I just want to be with you. Alone. The rest of the world can fuck right off."

"Babe!" Judy hugs Darren tightly. She didn't want the moment to end either. It was perfect. But the thing about a moment, no matter how perfect, is that it has to pass. And life is always in motion. She glances at her watch while hugging him. It was past 10. "Babe, don't you need to head to work?"

Darren takes a look at the time. "Oh, fuck! Yeah, I need to run,"

"Come over to mine afterwards?" asks Judy.

"Yes, love, I'll be there," Darren changes into his work clothes. "Just as soon as I'm done with work today, I'll come see my fiancée."

Judy blushes and smiles. Takes another gander at the ring on her finger. "I love this ring. Must have cost you a fortune. How long have you been saving up for this?"

Darren smiles, but his mind turns to another thought. One more thing he needed to come clean about: the 2 million. He couldn't hide that forever. He had also decided to quit his job at Flaming Nero's. With the 2 million, he could start something of his own. But all of this would have to wait. This moment was perfect for now. And too much honesty, like too much of anything, wasn't ideal. "I started saving for it the moment I knew you were the one. So, like a month into us dating."

"I love you, babe. But we need to discuss finances. We can't make such reckless expenses anymore. We have to live on a budget. We shouldn't go to France either. At least not now. Maybe for our honeymoon."

Darren feigns a smile. "Yes, of course. How about we leave tonight and disappear into the countryside instead? Get away from it all for a few days?" That would be enough time for the heat from Louie to subside. The countryside was as good as France.

Judy smiles. "I'd like that very much. Will you ask your mum as well?"

Darren holds her close. "I don't want to. I just want you."

She kisses him back but only briefly. "Babe, I think you should ask your mum to join us. We had a blast last night. She reminded me so much of my aunt. And I think it'll be good for the both of you."

Darren knew Judy was right. If he wanted a family, he would have to learn to tolerate his mum's overbearing nature. Moreover, he needed to get her away from danger as well. "You're right babe. I will call her. I know the three of us will have a fantastic time."

"I know Patricia and I will for sure. In fact, we're meeting in a bit to get our nails done." She shows him her bare nails. He kisses her hand.

"Alright love. Have fun. Don't believe any of the embarrassing stories she tells you about me."

"But those are the most fun to hear," Judy giggles. "For now, you should head to work. You're going to be late. And so will I. Don't want to keep your mum waiting."

Darren smiles and lets go of her. Walks out of his flat with a smile. He keeps imagining himself and Judy (and his mum) somewhere deep in the English countryside. In some cottage overlooking endless green farmlands. It had everything he ever wanted. His *perfect little family*. Peace. Stillness. Money. Maybe they could stay there for the rest of their lives. Maybe that's how "Plan B" is supposed to end. With the 2 million, it wasn't far-fetched at all. Or was it?

Darren knew he needed to think this through. He couldn't take another step without relieving this burden in his mind. Should he leave London? His heart kept telling him yes. Get out while you still can. With the money. That all made sense. The part that bothered him was the one that was telling him to leave London **forever**. But the more he listened to that side, the more he agreed with it.

"But what about Bob?" Came the other voice. You have to avenge him. But could he really? Could he stand up to Louie? He knew he couldn't. Mr Shadow? Well, Louie couldn't stand up to him. What chance did he have in all of this? But the other voice asked, "did chance really matter?" His honour for his friend was at stake. But his heart kept saying Plan B. Judy is more important than Bob. And Bob would understand his situation. Right? Then Darren realised the ultimate truth. It's what the other voice, his heart and his gut kept trying to tell him all along. He didn't care what Bob would have thought. He loved him. He was his best friend. But he was part of a world Darren wanted to leave behind. And that's what he really needed to do. Leave all of this behind. Maybe his worlds didn't need to collide.

But would Louie or Mr Shadow ever stop chasing him? He knew Louie wouldn't. Not unless he disappears. And in the countryside, he could do just that. But what about Mr Shadow? How long were his shadowy arms? Darren knew there was only one way to find out. Plan B.

The realisation that this could all be a reality very soon gave him the motivation he needed to see it through. He was convinced this was the right thing to do. He was going to fly the coop. He glances at the hallway light and its halo. It was perfect. It was angelic. Maybe it was a sign from God that he was doing the right thing. Maybe there was a bit of faith in him after all.

— CHAPTER 21 —

So What Will You Two Have?

"It's the number of that pizza place with the doughnut-shaped pizzas. Flaming Nero's," answers Dave as he hangs up the phone.

"That's quite close to Mr Shadow's lair. And he did call that number several times. Once well past midnight," adds Riley. "You think maybe he just loves their pizza?"

"No, no! That can't be it. Whoever was on the other end of those calls is someone Mr Shadow trusts implicitly," Dave ponders as his stomach begs to be fed. "I think we should grab a bite to eat."

"How can you think about food at a time like this?" An annoyed Riley was bursting at the seams, raring to go.

"Because we'll be more rational with a full stomach. And we can't make any stupid, silly mistakes. We need to handle this just right. Our lives are at stake. And so is the money."

Riley still wasn't convinced. Finally, they had a clue to work on. To stop dead in their tracks now was foolish as far as he was concerned.

"And I am craving a doughnut-shaped pizza," Dave smiles deviously.

Riley finally understands. He smiles back. "Now that you mention it, I am starving too. And a doughnut-shaped pizza does sound perfect."

"And I know just the place. It's a short walk away."

"Then lead the way, kind sir," Riley beckons Dave as he takes out another cigarette.

The dynamic duo walk as fast as they could to reach Flaming Nero's. Even so, it was a good 20-minute walk. It would have taken 10 minutes according to Riley if Dave didn't keep stopping and complaining about shortness of breath.

Riley suggested that he eat healthier and start a workout routine, but his helpful advice only earned him a flurry of insults and lectures on how the "youth" don't respect elders anymore. Dave was a year older than Riley. They were both in their twenties.

Dave doubled down on his offence by telling Riley that he shouldn't smoke. That's what was truly unhealthy. While Dave was correct, Riley did counter back with a mic drop moment. He said at least he wasn't feeling any shortness of breath.

That should have ended the conversation right then and there. But Dave wasn't done. He picked up the mic Riley had dropped and kept talking into it anyway. He wanted to have the last laugh. Riley just wanted quiet time.

All Dave's constant blabbering did was give Riley a headache, the opposite of what he wanted. The upside was that he didn't feel like smoking anymore. So as far as Dave was concerned, he had won. He had the last laugh. He was the one who dropped the mic last. Riley just wanted breakfast and conceded defeat. Anything was acceptable to him as long as Dave would shut the hell up. The last few minutes of their walk were spent in silence. Glorious silence. So, in Riley's mind he had won. He had the last laugh (Insert Mic Drop.gif).

They reach Flaming Nero's and take in the establishment with all its glory. The piss-poor excuse for a restaurant with its terrible food and worse ambience somehow kept thriving. It was a perfect metaphor for England as far as Dave was concerned. They were both now ravenously hungry. Their last meal was Wendy's which was over 12 hours ago. Riley was ready to head inside, but Dave stood with his feet firmly planted on the ground reading the menu on the display window.

"They have the same menu inside. And you could ask them what the specials are," Riley was impatient and hangry.

"Settle down, pup. I want to be sure of what I want to order. Or at least know what my preferences are. I don't want to hold the line up."

"It's 10.30 in the fucking morning and this place isn't run by the Soup Nazi. Look, it's almost empty. You can chew the ear of the man behind the counter. Now let's please fucking go. I need to eat or I'll go mental," Riley pleads with Dave.

It worked. They both entered Flaming Nero's and looked around at the garish decor of the establishment.

"Would you look at this place?" says Riley, disgusted.

"I know! It's smashing. We should have come here sooner," replies Dave. And he wasn't kidding. He really did love it. Dave was an arsonist after all.

Riley looks at him with some amount of contempt. "Let's just fucking order and see what we can find out."

Dave walks to the counter where he sees the employee wearing an apron with his back towards him. He rings the bell to get his attention. The employee turns around, and it's Darren. Dave is taken aback. So is Darren.

Riley hadn't seen Darren yet. He was busy scanning the menu. "Hi, can I have the beef and pesto doughnut supreme and…" He realises the uncomfortable silence that had surrounded him. And then realises why. "Darren! What the fuck are you doing here?"

Darren was embarrassed. He never told the crew he worked here because it was… well, embarrassing. Especially the stupid fucking apron. "I work here."

"Since when?" asks Dave. His mind was running a million miles a minute. It's the place Mr Shadow kept calling over and over again. And who was working here? Darren! Their friend and cohort. The one they had begun to suspect. It seems their suspicions were not out of place.

"Since I got out of prison," replies Darren.

"Why didn't you ever tell us?" asks Riley, whose anger was getting harder to contain. His mind was also racing with the different possibilities. And they all said the same thing. Their friend had betrayed them.

Darren was just embarrassed. No other thought crossed his mind. "Look around."

Dave and Riley are confused. But they do.

Darren continues. "Look at this stupid apron I'm wearing. I was embarrassed. The pair of you are in construction. And Bob was a courier. This job sucks in comparison. And have you seen this fucking apron?"

Nick, the establishment's owner, walks by at this very moment. "Watch your tongue, Turner, or it'll be your last day working here."

"Yes, Nick," responds Darren glibly. He already knew it was his last day. He looks at his fellow gang members. "So what would you two like to eat? Most of this is terrible if I'm being honest."

Nick steps out of his cabin. "Turner! Get in here. NOW!"

"As soon as I'm done taking this order," Darren turns to Dave and Riley. "So what will you two have?"

Riley's fists were clenching, his teeth were grinding, his blood was boiling, you get the picture. He was about to pounce on Darren then and there.

Dave agrees every bit with this sentiment, but he knows they have to play their cards right. He speaks out before Riley can react. "No, we're good. Not really that hungry now that I think about it, we'll see you in a bit mate. Cheerio!" He pulls Riley away back outside the restaurant against his will, leaving a very confused Darren behind.

Darren walks into Nick's cabin and is greeted by yelling. He retorts by yelling back.

Outside, Dave tries to calm Riley down but to no avail.

Riley was just flabbergasted. "The wanker's in on it. Let's go cave his fucking skull in right now."

Dave responds. "Patience. We don't know the whole story yet."

Riley retorts. "What else do we need to fucking know? It's clear as day. He fucking betrayed us. All the signs point to him." Riley was hyperventilating. He takes out a cigarette to calm himself down. Offers one to Dave, who declines.

"We can't see the forest yet from the trees. Trust me. I'm on your side but we need to think this through. Not do anything stupid." Dave responds.

Inside the restaurant, an angry Darren throws his apron at Nick, who cusses him out. Darren shows him the finger. Nick throws a pot, which Darren narrowly manages to avoid.

Outside, Dave and Riley continue their conversation.

"Then what do you fucking suggest? Suck him off and let bygones be bygones?" Riley demands to know from Dave.

Dave empathises with Riley. He really does. He too wants answers to the never-ending list of questions they have about their predicament. But attacking Darren here wasn't the answer. "Look! I don't know what the right thing to do is. I really don't. But if you want my suggestion, I feel like we should go someplace for breakfast and talk things through. Figure out what we really need to do. I need to eat. Otherwise, this anger is going to consume me like it has you and then we'll end up reacting emotionally. Not rationally. That's not what Bob taught us to do. And we need to heed his advice especially now."

Riley doesn't like what Dave said but he knows he is right. Especially the part about Bob. He begrudgingly nods in agreement. "You're right.

But if we find out this cunt has betrayed us, then I am going to pull the trigger on him."

"And I will hold him down for you." Dave responds. They were finally in agreement. "Let's be on our way then. We have a lot to do and no time to lose."

Riley tosses his cigarette and the pair of them leave Flaming Nero's to find a more suitable place for breakfast.

Moments later, Darren exits the restaurant and looks up at the heavens as if he's a free man. He felt the same way when he got out of prison. He now had to rush home, pack his bags and the money and head to Judy's. They were going to leave London tonight. Plan B was in motion. Plan B was now his life.

COCKTAIL DRESS, FISHNET STOCKINGS AND HIGH HEELS

In Holborn, inside the cabin of a ground floor office that was nothing short of a brick armoured fortress on a corner plot with no sign to be found, sat three nervous people. They were Gareth, Lloyd, and Ginger.

Gareth was tall and wiry and wore circular-rimmed glasses. He looked a bit like an older Harry Potter on meth. This tough son of a bitch had won more fistfights than Muhammad Ali and could probably have taken him down in his prime. But at this moment, he was closer to shitting his pants than an actual baby.

Lloyd was short and stocky. He wore a hat to hide his balding hair. He wasn't very quick on his feet or the sharpest saw in the toolshed. But he did have the sharpest eyesight among those on the wrong side of the law. It made him the best marksman money could buy in all of London. And he could more than handle himself in a fight. You didn't want to be on the other side of

Lloyd in a bar brawl. But at this moment, he was sweating uncontrollably and almost sobbing like a schoolgirl with a freshly bruised kneecap.

Ginger was short, skinny, had tattoos all over her arms, and had bright red hair. She had a stripper's body and manners worse than one. She was a pretty sight to look at, except when you saw her yellow, decaying teeth brought on by years of chewing tobacco. But if you ever told her that she needed to see a dentist, she would cut you into a million pieces with her knives, of which she hid plenty in her leather pants and low-cut punk rock t-shirts. But at this moment, she was shaking like a vibrator stuck on max speed. Never in her life had she ever felt this way. She chewed gum to counteract the anxiety and restlessness. But it made no difference. Her phone gets a text message. She gingerly picks it up and reads. Slowly, a smile spreads across her face. She stops shaking like a vibrator being turned off from max speed.

They were all seated on one side of a large table and were waiting. Waiting for the person who would sit on the other side to show up. It was almost 11 am. All 3 of them got a text message an hour ago that the big guy wanted to see them.

He wanted updates. The kind of updates that at least two of them did not have.

The door behind them swings open. They don't turn around, but the tension is palpable among Gareth and Lloyd. Ginger sits there blowing bubbles with her chewing gum. POP goes the bubble and is instantly replaced by the clickety-clack sound of high heels walking behind them and then around them.

The tip of the heels left some drops of blood behind on the floor. Gareth knew where that blood came from. He had seen it before. He didn't want his blood to end up on those heels. To make sure of that, all he had to do was answer truthfully and have faith in the big man above. Not God. But the wearer of those high heels was now standing right in front of them across the table.

It was a 50-year-old man with long grey hair, who was tougher than a coffin nail, who stood with a glower that could melt stone. He was dressed in an expensive cocktail dress, fishnet stockings, and high heels with which he would beat you to death if you so much as happened to call him a fruitcake. In his own words, he was fabulous and all man. That's what he also said to the men he had his way with. Sometimes consensually, sometimes not.

This was Louie James. To the world, a high street fashion designer, but that was just a front. His actual work was supplying most of Europe with the best ecstasy and cocaine money and influence could buy. And what's better than your fashion weeks to directly reach a very wealthy clientele? The answer to that rhetorical question is nothing.

Louie sits down comfortably in front of the three of them and eyes them like bugs to be crushed under his heel. You did not want to be on this man's bad side. He opens his purse to take out some sketches he had been working on. Underneath them was a severed finger he's half-surprised to find. He picks it up and looks at it confused. He wondered who did it belong to? He notices Gareth and Lloyd were disturbed by this and were avoiding looking him in the eye. But Ginger sat with ease and looked straight at him. He liked that. At least one of his people wasn't afraid of him. He needed people who could be honest with him. Like Ginger and Matt. But Matt was untraceable at the moment. These three are all he had for now and they'd have to do.

He tosses the finger nonchalantly into the bin and turns his gaze on the three of them.

"So do you have any updates about who murdered the love of my life, killed my assistant in cold blood, stole 5 million quid from me and burned my house to the fucking ground? SPEAK!" roared Louie.

Gareth was twitching uncontrollably. He did not have any updates to share. "No! No, I don't. I'm... I'm sorry," he says meekly and looks away. He was taking slow, deep breaths to try and stay calm. It wasn't working well.

Lloyd does better, but only slightly. He struggles to say every word and stumbles at every other. But he does manage to string together a full sentence. "Well... Actually... I've been asking around... And the... The thing is... No! I've found nothing." He also looks away from Louie's gaze.

Louie wasn't happy hearing this, but he expected it. Gareth and Lloyd had their uses, but solving crimes wasn't one of them. They were hardcore fighters and killers. The ones with brawn. Not brains. He turns to Ginger. "Ginger! I hope you've brought some sunshine on this very cloudy day."

Ginger blows a bubble from her chewing gum, and it pops. "Of course I did, Louie."

Louie smiles. "Good girl. What have you got?"

"I got an ID from the Bobbys on the bloke who had some of our stolen money. Found out from my network that he ran a crew with three other people. Details on two of them were Slim Pickens at best. Maybe they're that good or that green. But one of his crew mates was a member of the Tower Hamlets crew that used to nick cars from Waterloo and Southwark. The ones that created all the fuss in 02."

Louie was unimpressed. "That's all you've got? There's got to be more. I've had to pull a lot of strings and pay a lot of money to keep my name away from the press. But there's only so much I can do. Sooner or later, all of this will break and then we'll be powerless to do anything. Is this all you've been able to find?" Louie was irate.

Lloyd and Gareth look worried. The only thought on their mind was that Louie's high heels would meet their skull next.

Ginger was still cool as a cucumber. She blows another bubble and waits for it to pop. "It was looking like that, but things turned around a corner right before you got here. One of my people was able to meet up with one of those former Tower Hamlets boys who ran with him. It took a little persuasion, but he was able to beat a name out of him.

Louie was now interested. "Well, let's hear the cunt's name."

"David Moore. Goes by Dave. Spent 3 years in the clink for arson and grand theft auto. But that's not all."

Louie smiles. "Colour me interested. Don't keep me waiting, love."

"I have an address."

Louie has a big grin on his face now.

"I was just waiting for you to get here to let you know that I'm going to be paying him a visit." Ginger takes out one of her knives and admires it. "And I'm going to cut him open with this unless he tells me where the rest of his gang is. Get you a matching finger for the one you already have." She sheathes it back.

Louie was happy with Ginger's update. "Someone's getting their Christmas bonus early this year."

"You can double it instead." She gives Louie a cheeky smile and gets up to leave. "I'm off. I'll be back with your money and the fingers of those who decided to cross you. Cheerio!"

"Wait!" Louie says authoritatively. Ginger stops at the door. "Take Dumb and Dumber with you." Louie gestures for Gareth and Lloyd to go with her.

Ginger wasn't happy hearing this, and it was visible on her face just like that one pimple she swears 'just won't go away'. "I can handle this by myself."

"Of course you can. But they might come in handy. A strong cock needs two firm balls by its side." Louie turns his attention to the boys. "Follow her lead. Do everything she says. Don't disappoint me like you have already." Louie gestures them to leave. He begins to peruse the sketches he had taken out from his purse.

Gareth and Lloyd nod and get up in a hurry. They follow Ginger outside and get into a car. Ginger sits in the back, Lloyd takes shotgun, and Gareth gets behind the wheel.

"Where are we heading, Ginger?" Lloyd asks while putting a silencer on his gun.

"Mile End. And step on it. I have dinner plans which I don't intend to miss," she says sharply as she blows another bubble.

— CHAPTER 23 —

Is Anybody Home?

Ginger, Lloyd and Gareth reach Mile End. Weekend rush ensured they didn't have a parking spot available for miles on end. Ginger tells Gareth to stay close by behind the wheel. She and Lloyd would go and check Dave's flat out. They were expecting trouble, and it was important for them to get away fast in case things didn't go their way.

Ginger and Lloyd walk into the building with an air of confidence that could be mistaken for arrogance. They were ready for almost anything.

Lloyd kept his gun locked and loaded in his coat pocket. He didn't even need to take it out to fire the first shot. It was already pointing forward. And with the silencer attached, it was the perfect weapon to strike first and discreetly.

Ginger carried a gun too but preferred using her knives. She felt it was a lot more personal. And she loved to see the life leave her victims' eyes when she took it from them. It turned her on.

She always needed a shag after a killing. That's what her dinner plan was.

Their confidence was slightly dampened when they read the sign: "Lift out of order." Dave's flat was 5 floors up. But at least they didn't have to carry an unconscious man up with them like Darren and Riley. They quickly made their way up the stairs without delay. Ginger could run a marathon without breaking a sweat, and while Lloyd was on the heavier side and not the quickest on his feet, he had a certain nimbleness about him. He barely made a sound while walking.

They reach Dave's floor and wonder how they should proceed?

"I'll ring the doorbell and see if anyone's there. You be in position by the stairwell to take out any troublemaker," Ginger suggests.

"Whatever you say, Ginger. The big guy asked us to follow your lead. And we're going to do just that," Lloyd was more than happy for Ginger to make all these decisions. He just wanted to shoot someone. His trigger finger was itching. It had been days since he used his gun. He always celebrated a kill by drowning himself in rum and coke. Not Coca-Cola. And working with Louie, coke was always easy to come by. And top-tier stuff at that. None of that stuff mixed with baking powder or other adulterants.

Ginger rings the doorbell and keeps one hand behind her back ready to take a knife out at a moment's notice. There is no response from inside. Not even a whisper. She counts in her head till 10 and rings the doorbell again. She waits for a response.

Lloyd stood in position as solid as a rock. He removed the lock from his pistol without taking it out. He knew his pistol better than he knew the back of his hand. Or even the front of his hand.

There was still no response. Nobody was home. Ginger gestures for Lloyd to join her. He reaches the door and takes a good, long look at it.

"You think you can jimmy it open?" asks Ginger.

"No, but Gareth can."

"Alright then. Call him up. I hope he's not too far away. Dave can return home at any moment."

Lloyd calls Gareth, and his phone begins to ring. He wasn't answering it, but they soon heard the ringer off in the distance, and it kept getting louder and louder. Gareth walks in from the stairwell and joins them. He was a little out of breath. Lloyd cuts the call.

"What are you doing here? I told you to wait in the car," barks Ginger.

Gareth was still steadying himself and catching his breath.

"But you just asked me to call him up here," interjects Lloyd.

Ginger was seething. "I did. But he came up before he was ordered to. That's not right. What if we were in trouble and needed to get away?" Ginger calms herself down. "Nevertheless, this does save us some time." She turns to Gareth. "Did you find a parking spot nearby?"

"Found one right outside. I was worried you guys were taking too long, so I decided to come take a look," says Gareth.

"And you came at just the right time. We need to get this door open. Take a gander at it, won't you, mate?" Lloyd tells Gareth.

Gareth was Darren's replacement in Louie's gang. And he was the perfect replacement. Opening safes and locks were child's play for him. And he was less of a pain in the arse compared to Darren if you ever asked Matt. Louie didn't care either way. As long as the work was done, it didn't matter who did the job. All of these employees were expendable to him. Lloyd and Ginger were newer hires as well. They had joined after Darren was locked up. Job security and longevity were not among the perks in Louie's employment. But access to a lot of easy money was. And a taste of the high life. And that attracted the right talent from all around.

Gareth takes a good look at the lock and takes out his tools. It takes him less than thirty seconds to get the door open. It swings open without making a sound. Dave made sure the hinges were well-oiled and taken care of. Like the rest of his flat.

They tentatively step in with their guns pointed forward. They were ready for anything. A minute later, they breathed a sigh of relief. The flat was empty.

"Let's see if this cunt has our money or not. Spread out and search," Ginger shouts her orders.

A few minutes of searching is all it took, and they found another million of the remaining 4. It was hidden well by Dave under many knick-knacks in a cabinet, but in a flat this small, it wasn't going to stay hidden for too long.

"Your people were right. Let's head back to the big guy with this. It'll surely bring a smile to his face," suggests Gareth.

"No!" replies Ginger. "Not yet! This means we're on the right track. We still have 3 million left to find. And this wanker knows exactly where the rest of it is. We wait here for him to return. He's not going to leave all this money behind for too long."

Lloyd and Gareth nod in agreement. And not just because of Louie's orders. She did have the right idea. Even if she conveyed it in the crudest, most hateful manner possible.

"Tea anyone?" Gareth asks them, and they both nod in the affirmative. They were, after all, English.

"I wonder where he is," says Lloyd as the three of them make themselves comfortable in Dave's flat.

A few miles away in Hackney, Dave and Riley reach Darren's flat. After a hale and hearty breakfast full of discussions, sausages, and mash, they both agreed to search Darren's home for further clues. With him being at work, it was the perfect time.

"We're here but how do we get inside?" enquires Dave. "Neither of us is good at lock picking."

Riley smiles his cheekiest smile. "Just so we have it, we're in luck." He takes out a key from inside his wallet. "Darren gave me a spare because I live close by. In case of an emergency."

Dave gets excited, grabs hold of Riley and kisses him on the lips.

"Settle down, mate," Riley shrugs and pushes Dave away not so gently.

"Sorry, bruv. It's the first thing that's gone our way all day."

Riley unlocks the door, and they enter.

"It's a studio so it shouldn't take too long to find anything."

Riley agreed and they began their short search, which lasted all of a few minutes.

"The money isn't here. But there are some files that he nicked from Mr Shadow's lair. And it clearly looks like he packed some of his clothes," Dave says.

"You think he flew the coop?"

Dave thinks about what Riley had said while his gaze was caught by a few letters that were addressed to Judy. He was about to say something to Riley but stops. Gets transfixed on a thought. Has flashes of Darren telling them that he wants to start a family and get away from it all. He moves from Judy's letters onto Darren's research notes from last night. Darren clearly spent a lot of time poring through those files. But it was clear he found nothing. And now his money was gone. So were his clothes. The signs were clear. Darren ran away. But why?

Riley snaps at Dave to get his attention. "Oye, Peter Pan. You think he flew off to Neverland?"

Dave thinks about what he wants to say. "Maybe. I'm thinking we should do the same. Get out of London with our money while we have the chance. Wait for all of this to blow over."

"What if it doesn't blow over?"

"Then we don't come back. We have the money to start over."

"What about Darren? Are we going to let him get away with this?"

"If he's flown the coop then there's not much we can do. Is there?"

"I guess not. It just doesn't feel right though. Bob's dead because of him."

"If he is responsible then you and I are next."

Riley was getting riled up again. "This is why we should have killed him when we had the chance. It'd be one less thing to worry about."

"But what if he's flown the coop because he wants to get Judy and his mum to safety. We're still not sure if he and Mr Shadow are in cahoots."

"What other proof do we need?" Riley barks back. "Mr Shadow called him multiple times. He didn't do that with any of us. One meeting was all it took."

"Does that really prove anything?"

"He took files from Mr Shadow's lair without telling us."

"And if you look at his notes, it's clear he's also trying to find Mr Shadow."

"Maybe if he put that there to trick us."

"Oh, for god's sake Riley, hear yourself."

Riley was still convinced Darren had betrayed them. "He said the same thing that Mr Shadow said. Why the antagonism?"

"So? They said the same thing. Maybe one of them copied the other. The explanation could be that simple."

Riley looks incredulously at Dave.

"Riles! Think about this. We're clutching at straws looking for something where there might be none. Maybe they're on the same side. Maybe they're not. Maybe our friend is just as scared as us and wants to take care of the people he loves. I'm not sure. We really don't know anything. And that's the truth."

Riley hated to admit it, but what Dave said was making sense to him. He just hadn't completely accepted it yet. He needed a vessel to direct his anger to. And Darren was an easy one. "Then what would you have us to do?"

Dave was conflicted with his decision to run away as well. But the outcome mattered more to him than getting revenge. He just needed Riley to see things his way. "I want to ask you one thing. And be honest with your answer."

"Ask away."

"Would you rather find out the truth in all of this or keep the money and run away?"

"Why does it have to be one or the other?"

"Because honestly… We don't have it in us to find Mr Shadow and take down Louie."

"What do you mean we don't?" This offended Riley. He had complete faith that they could.

"Because we simply don't. Mr Shadow was able to plan the perfect revenge against someone as powerful as Louie James. Make him look like a complete patsy, We're nobodies in comparison."

"We're not nobodies." Riley was too stubborn to admit their shortcomings.

"You're right. We're not nobodies. We're the somebodies that Louie will take revenge on. And we both know it's coming.

Realisation hit Riley harder than he imagined. But he was thankful that it did. Because it made his choice easy. And before they did anything stupid. He takes a deep breath before speaking. "You're right. We should fly the coop. I want to avenge

Bob's murder and find out who Mr Shadow is. But not at the cost of my life or the money. It sucks to say it. I feel like a horrible person. But it is the truth."

Dave nods. "That's exactly how I feel."

"So, it's decided then. I'm heading over to my flat to get my bag."

"Wait!"

Riley stops in his tracks. Dave takes out his car keys and tosses them to Riley, who catches them better than most English slip fielders.

"Take my car and meet me back at mine. Don't carry your bag without a car."

"You're right, mate. Thanks! But how are you going to get home?"

"I'll take the bus or a cab. Just come get me at mine. We'll leave together from there."

"But where do you reckon we should go?"

Dave thinks about it deeply but not for too long. He already had the answer in his mind. "I've always wanted to have the finest scotch in the land. And I want it fresh out of the cask."

Riley smiles. "And I've always wanted to try some haggis. I guess I'll be checking that off the bucket list real soon."

He leaves to go get his money. Dave takes one last look at Darren's flat. He picks up one of Judy's letters, which had her address on it. He pockets it.

CHAPTER 24

Operation "Fly the Coop"

Riley tosses his bag of money onto the passenger seat while getting inside Dave's car. He opens the bag ever so slightly just to make sure the money is all still there. It is. He smiles as his eyes gleam. They are so close to getting away with it all. He zips the bag shut and keeps it close to him. Has the long strap clasped around his hand while he holds onto the gearshift. He isn't going to let the bag go out of his sight. Not even for a moment. He turns the car on and commences his commute to Dave's.

The stereo was preset to BBC Radio 1, which was blasting Gary Glitter's greatest hits. Why? No one knows for sure. The top theory was that the BBC Radio 1 DJ loved Glitter's music and vehemently believed in separating the art from the artist, even if the said artist diddled children. He was fired shortly after this incident.

Riley wasn't a part of the "Glitterati" and decides to peruse Dave's CD collection instead. He finds a case of his music collection in the glove box. He places it on his lap and takes a gander at it while driving. The first CD was Celine Dion's greatest hits. Riley assumes it belonged to an ex. He turns over and finds Whitney Houston's first 2 albums. He's in disbelief as he flips through the entire case and only finds Cher, Madonna, and Barry Manilow.

"Where the fuck is your Metallica and Megadeth?" Riley yells in a fit of rage and hits the steering wheel. He realises he's jumped a traffic light while being distracted. He swerves at the last minute to avoid hitting a pedestrian who was shouting obscenities at him and giving him the finger. Riley looks back and breathes a sigh of relief.

"Gary Glitter will do just fine," he says to himself and tosses the CD case aside. He begins humming along to "Do You Wanna Touch Me" while imagining that it was probably written for some nine-year-old Glitter wanted to be touched by. After a few minutes of cautious driving, he finally calms down. He picks up his phone to call Dave…

… Who was slowly but surely making his way up the 5 flights of stairs. His phone begins to ring, so he stops to catch his breath. Sees it's Riley and answers it straight away. "Yeah, Riles."

"I'm almost there. Got my bag with me. Scotland here we fucking come." Riley was in a booming mood. He was excited about the life they had ahead of them. The possibilities and outcomes were endless. And they had the money to do almost whatever they wanted. Riley imagined himself opening a homely pub on a quiet street corner and ending each day of hard work with a nice cold pint of Guinness.

"I'm just climbing up the stairs. They're finally fixing the lift but I couldn't wait a moment longer. I'll see you downstairs in about 5." Dave takes a deep breath. Gathers some energy and exuberance. "Scotland, let's fucking go!" He wanted to match Riley's level of enthusiasm because he was at that level too. But climbing up the stairs had knocked some of it out of him. He too had already decided what he was going to do with his money: open an off licence with a cashpoint. No safer bet in his mind.

"Perfect, bruv. I'll see you then." Riley cuts the call and begins to sing along to "I'm the leader of the gang (I am)." He had started coming around to Gary Glitter. He had learned to separate the art from the artist. Thank you, BBC Radio 1 DJ.

Dave is on the verge of collapsing by the time he reaches his floor. "Fuck! Riley's right. I really need to start taking care of myself." He pulls himself up with the dado rail. "To working out and eating right in Scotland. But also ending each day with scotch fresh out of the cask." He was manifesting this in his mind.

He takes a few moments to gather himself. Takes a look at his hallway. Everything was in its right place but something didn't quite feel right. Something felt off. Maybe it was last-minute jitters as they decided to flee London without any notice. But it was also the right thing to do. Even if it meant leaving this life behind. A life in Scotland with the money they had had the potential of being a more fulfilling existence than their current life. Even if it meant starting over without a hand-woven carpet from Kashmir. Dave realises he's overthinking things. He just needed to grab his bag of money and leave as soon as possible. He takes out his key and unlocks the door.

He opens it and sees his home just as he left it. He smiles, taking one last look at it. It had been his home for almost three years, and he was proud of it. He had truly made it someplace he was always happy to return to at the end of the day. He takes a deep breath and enters one last time. A few steps in, and he sees everything is normal. He wondered why he felt something was off? And then he learns what his gut was trying to tell him. He is greeted by a gun to the back of his head.

It was Lloyd. "Welcome home, mate. We've been expecting you."

Dave turns around slowly to take a look at the man pointing the gun at him. He was now looking straight down the barrel. He puts his hands behind his head and slowly takes a few steps back. Lloyd watches him closely. Dave was doing his best to stay calm, but his heart was racing at a million miles a minute. He had never fired a gun or killed anyone. And he certainly never had a gun pointed at him. He had, however, been stabbed a couple of times. This was London after all.

"Where's the rest of our money?" Lloyd asks calmly.

"I don't know," Dave lies bravely. He didn't know he had it in him. He always imagined himself folding faster than laundry if he was ever confronted by Louie's men.

"Don't you dare lie to me, you son of a bitch. We'll find out one way or another."

"OH, YOU FUCKING CUNT!" Dave's neighbour yells out like he usually did during his football match. This startles Lloyd, who glances away at the source of the sound momentarily. It was long enough for Dave to take out his own gun and point it back at Lloyd.

"Drop your gun or I'll pump you full of lead," Dave thought he had dropped a cool one-liner from an action film, but he hadn't. It was massively derivative. Either way, it didn't matter. The odds were evened out.

Lloyd smiles. "Finally. Someone with fucking balls."

"I'll make this simple for you. I'm going to walk out of here. You keep the money you've found. And we forget this ever happened. How does that sound?"

"That is truly very generous of you. But luckily I brought backup."

Gareth walks out of the bedroom with a gun of his own pointed at Dave. "I'd put that gun down if I were you."

Dave sees the predicament he's in. Both Lloyd and Gareth are calm and collected. They are professionals who have done this many times before. They wear gloves and have silencers on their guns. They'll kill him and leave without anyone knowing any better. All Dave wants to do is to tell Riley to run. Save himself from this. At least he could have the life he always dreamed of. He sees no way out for himself. This will be the place where he dies. He begins lowering his gun but then stops. He has a thought. A crazy one. But it is better than doing nothing. If this is the time and place he dies, then he will make one final stand. He is not going down without a fight. He points his gun right back at Lloyd.

"What are you thinking?" Lloyd asks him. "Have you gone absolutely bonkers?"

Dave smiles manically. "I'm thinking I'll be dead either way. Might as well take one of you cunts with me."

The moment is tense. Who will take the first shot? Who would blink first? No one wanted this to turn into a bloodbath. But the chances of it being anything else were slim to none.

Dave blinks first, but he does the unexpected. He lunges at Gareth and takes him by surprise.

Gareth drops his gun in the process. They roll on the floor trying to land blows on each other.

Lloyd couldn't get a clear shot at Dave. "Gareth, hold him steady so I can take him out," he yells.

Dave hits Gareth in the face with his gun, leaving him bruised and bloody. Gareth tries his best to reach for his gun, which was ever so slightly out of reach. He stretches as far as he can and manages to hold onto the grip. Dave smacks Gareth's hand, preventing him from grasping his gun properly. He then steadies himself to take aim and shoot Gareth.

This gives Lloyd a clear shot at Dave. He cocks his gun and is about to shoot when, at that precise moment, Gareth overpowers Dave and tosses him aside. Dave's gun slides away well out of everyone's reach. Gareth pins him to the ground and punches him hard repeatedly in the face. Lloyd no longer had a clear shot at Dave, but at least Gareth was in control.

He chokes Dave with both his hands. Dave strikes Gareth back repeatedly with his right hand, but it makes no difference other than adding to Gareth's annoyance. He takes Dave's right arm and pins it down with his knee. Dave was going nowhere and now had no way to fight back. He was struggling and gasping for air. This was a hundred times worse than climbing up 5 flights of stairs. Gareth looks him in the eye with a sadistic pleasure, wanting to watch Dave's soul leave his body.

This is how he was going to die. The realisation set in Dave's mind. His left hand was free, but it was bruised and hurt. No hit from it would slow Gareth down. He was losing the will to fight back. He was slowly accepting his fate. Death didn't seem so bad. It would be eternal peace. He slowly begins closing his eyes and letting it all go.

But then something catches the corner of his eye. It was Gareth's gun shining brightly on the floor. It had caught a bit of stray sunlight seeping in through the open window. It shone like an angel's halo. It felt like a sign from God. "Don't give up. Not yet."

He closes his eyes momentarily and recites a prayer in his mind. He gathers all the strength he could muster and lunges himself towards the gun. It works! He's able to grab it from the barrel and uses it like a club to land one clean powerful blow on Gareth's jaw. He gave it everything he had and is able to knock Gareth off him. Dave is now free. He pushes himself up. With blurry vision, he shoots at them blindly.

Lloyd grabs hold of Gareth. "Let's get out of here."

Gareth gets up and rushes out with him. The bullets barely miss them.

Dave tries to steady himself. His vision was still distorted. He knew he was not out of danger yet. He hears footsteps approaching his flat. *They're coming back*, he thinks to himself. The flat door swings open and without a moment to waste, he shoots at the target best he can. One bullet hits the intruder right in the gut. Dave hears him scream in pain and watches him fall to the ground.

He smiles and breathes a sigh of relief. He was going to get out of this alive. His vision slowly comes back into focus, and he takes a good look at his would-be killer.

He immediately regrets what he sees and rubs his eyes in disbelief. "No, this can't be happening." It was Riley. He had shot Riley in the gut. He lay there bleeding to death, screaming in pain and agony. His bag of money was beside him. But he didn't even hold onto it anymore. It didn't matter. Nothing did.

Dave starts bawling like a child. "No! No! This can't be." He goes to comfort Riley.

Riley looks at him with kind eyes while gasping for air.

"I'm so sorry. I didn't know it was you. Louie sent these two men. They had guns pointed at me. They took my money. I'm so sorry. I'm so sorry, Riley. Please stay with me. Don't you leave me. Stay with me." Dave keeps apologising over and over again.

Riley musters all the strength he has and manages to speak. "Fly… The… Coop." He hands Dave his money bag. With those final words, he lets go of his pain and accepts the sweet comforting embrace of death. He dies with a smile on his face, imagining pouring himself a nice cold pint of Guinness. He was finally at peace.

Dave shuts Riley's eyes and mutters a small prayer under his breath. He breaks down again, bawling and screams in anger.

Dave's neighbour had just about enough of this ruckus. He opens his door to yell, "WILL YOU SHUT THE FUCK UP?!" He sees Dave and Riley and freaks out. Takes a step back and falls to the floor in shock. He takes out his cellphone from his pocket.

Dave points his gun at him and shoots him without thinking. He takes out his car keys from Riley's pocket and grabs the bag of money. He runs down the stairs without looking back and exits the building.

Sits in his car and takes a deep breath. He still had tears running down his face. Calms himself down and turns the car on. BBC Radio 1 was still playing Gary Glitter. He turns the music down and thinks about what he's going to do next. He could leave for Scotland but with Riley dead it was only a matter of time before they got to Darren. He had to warn him about Louie, but he also couldn't trust him. But he was also his friend.. Dave wasn't sure on what to do next. He takes out Judy's letter from his coat pocket and reads her address. It was in Stratford. That was nearby. Could Darren be over there? Where else would he be if not at his own home? He thinks deeply about what he was going to do next. But he only thinks for a moment. He didn't have the luxury of time on his side. He knew in his heart what was the right thing to do and it had to be done. For Riley's sake. He drives off without wasting another breath.

A few parked cars down were Gareth, Lloyd, and Ginger. Lloyd hands Gareth a spare gun as they wait for Dave to leave. They follow him at a safe distance and wonder where he would lead them next. Most probably to the rest of his crew and the money they had stolen. This was going to end today.

CHAPTER 25

THE WHOLE TRUTH

Darren is with Judy at her flat. Judy rented a one-bedroom in a brand-new building that barely had any occupancy. The estate agents said it was only a matter of time before the lease doubled in price since East London was the new South London, just like how West London was a decade ago. They're just about done packing their suitcases in her bedroom. Among them was the duffel bag with the 2 million.

"I'm just going to hop in the shower real-quick. We can leave right after," Judy tells him.

"Alright, love. I'm waiting," he blows an affectionate kiss to her.

She smiles and steps inside her en suite washroom.

Darren waits for the washroom door to close completely and then opens the duffel bag to make sure the money was all still there. The entire gang did the same thing over and over again. It was still hard for them to believe that the money was real. Nothing seemed real since they got it. Well, except Bob getting brutally murdered. Darren did feel a pang of hatred towards himself for leaving London before finding out who was responsible for Bob's demise. But the decision he had made was the correct one. And he kept telling himself that. He just wasn't sure if he believed it. The other voice was still gnawing at him.

But then there were the counter arguments. A countryside life with Judy and his mum was as perfect as a life he could ever dream of. Being with the people he loved and among the peace he ever so desired. He was never going to get that in London. With Bob dead, it was only a matter of time before death showed up at his doorstep.

The doorbell rings, breaking his train of thought. "Who could that be at the doorstep?" he says to himself and goes to check.

Dave parks his car a stone's throw away from Judy's flat. It was the closest spot he could find. He grabs hold of what is now his bag of money and rushes inside.

He keeps turning around to see if he was being followed by Lloyd or Gareth. Luckily, they were nowhere to be found. There was just a cute redhead in a punk rock t-shirt who had entered the building right after him. She smiled at Dave when he eyed her suspiciously. Dave didn't think twice about her afterwards. I mean, he did, but not suspiciously. He was sure that she was a resident of these flats. She looked and dressed like an East Londoner for sure.

Judy's flat was on the second floor, and the lift was right at the top. Dave wasn't going to waste a moment. He ran up the stairs followed by the redhead, who walked casually behind him perusing through "her" mail.

Ginger keeps a close eye on Dave without raising his suspicions. She walks at a slow, steady pace. Behind a large envelope, she preps her gun out of Dave's sight, attaches a silencer, and makes sure that the clip is full. She is ready to make her move.

Dave reaches Judy's floor and finds her flat. He double-checks the address to make sure he's at the right place. He was. He rings the bell.

Darren opens the door and sees a broken and bruised Dave, who breathes a sigh of relief.

Darren was mostly happy to see him but was confused about why and how Dave found him here. He also wanted to ask why he looked like he had been beaten within an inch of his death.

He was just about to ask these very questions when Dave pulls a gun on him with tears in his eyes.

"Tell me the truth, Darren. Were you in on it from the start?"

Darren doesn't understand any of it. "In on it on what? I don't know what you're talking about, Dave. Why are you pointing a gun at me?" He raises his hands. "Did I do something wrong?"

Dave has tears running down his face. "Don't make this harder than it is. Were you in on it from the start? TELL ME! For Riley's sake."

"I honestly have no idea what you're talking about, Dave; I really don't. What happened to Riley? Where is he? Is he alright?"

Dave breaks down crying. He shakes his head.

Darren can't believe it. He tears up as well and holds the doorframe to stop himself from falling. First, it was Bob. Now Riley. Darren just wanted to be woken from this nightmare. He wanted to go back to the dream with him and Judy in Hyde Park. His life before that phone call.

Dave was never completely sure that Darren had double-crossed them. But now he was sure that Darren hadn't. He lowers his gun. "They're onto us down, Darren. Louie's people."

"Come inside. Tell me what happened. You look like you're an inch from death…" Darren had just said these words when Dave unexpectedly fell on him.

"Dave! Mate! Are you alright?" Dave wasn't. And Darren soon learns why. Dave was shot in the back of his head, and the bullet had lodged itself deep inside his brain. Darren's eyes light up in fear.

Ginger rushes inside and attacks a blindsided Darren. She pins him to the ground and chokes him with her hands. "Where's the money?"

Darren was still in shock at what had transpired. Now he was having flashbacks to the night when he killed someone for the first time. He hadn't processed Dave being killed in front of him or Riley's death, but now he was thrust into a struggle between life and death. He had his gun on him, but Ginger was choking the life out of him. To get free from her iron-like grip was first on the to-do list. He grabbed hold of her hands and used all his strength to pull them apart. He was seething with rage. He headbutted her twice, causing her nose to bleed. He readied his fist for a punch, but Ginger blocked it quite easily. It took all her strength, but she was able to overpower him again.

Gareth and Lloyd enter Judy's flat with Dave's bag of money. Ginger turns to them to give her orders. This diversion gives Darren the opportunity to sock her with a jab. She turns back to Darren and slaps him hard, proceeding to scratch him with her nails. He screams out in anguish.

"I've got this cunt locked down. Check the bedroom for the money. Kill anyone who gets in the way." Ginger barks out her orders as usual.

Gareth and Lloyd enter the bedroom. Lloyd places his gun on the bedside table to search more freely.

Gareth sifts through the dressers while Lloyd empties the packed suitcases on the bed. He peruses the contents, tossing articles of clothing aside, with one of them falling on his gun and obscuring it from his view.

He unzips the duffel bag and screams out in excitement. "FOUND THE MONEY!"

Ginger hears this and smiles. She punches Darren in the face.

Judy steps out of the washroom in a towel and is shocked to find two strange men in her bedroom going through her belongings. She reacts exactly as you'd expect her to. She screams at the top of her voice and draws their attention.

Gareth points his gun at her and she stops screaming. "No funny business, love."

Lloyd searches for his gun but can't seem to find it. However, Judy sees it. It was right next to her on the bedside table with a bit of it protruding out. And most importantly, it was out of their sight. All she needed was a distraction.

Outside in the living room, Darren and Ginger were still throwing hands at each other. Though they were more evenly matched, Ginger was getting the better of him. She punched him in the gut and kicked him in the groin. He fell down to his knees.

She takes out her favourite knife and taunts him. "Get up. I said, get up, you fucking wanker!"

Darren punches her squarely in the jaw knocking out one of her yellow teeth. She screams out in agony.

Inside the bedroom, Ginger's scream draws Gareth and Lloyd's gaze away from Judy. They wonder if Ginger needed their help.

A rush of insanity takes hold of Judy. She sees her moment. She knows what needs to be done. It is the only way she'll get out alive. Fight or flight! She picks up Lloyd's gun and shoots them both until the clip runs out. Each bullet riddles their bodies. No shot is wasted. They are both dead before they even hit the ground. This is the first time Judy has ever used a gun. Surprising considering she is American. But she is a natural, and her aim is impeccable. Not surprising since she is American.

She drops the gun in shock. She had no idea what came over her. She's shocked to see Darren's duffel bag is full of money. Her hands were trembling. She starts to freak out. She still wasn't sure if all this was happening or some bad dream she's found herself in. She snaps back to reality when she hears Darren screaming for his life.

Darren had been pushed up against the wall. He had lesions all over his face and body. His lip was bleeding profusely. Ginger puts her knife up against his throat.

"I'm going to enjoy cutting you up into little pieces. You'll soon be with all your friends." She has a fiendish smile on her face.

Judy steps out of her bedroom, sees them and shrieks out in terror. "DARREN! NO!"

Ginger turns to her. Darren seizes the opportunity and headbutts her with all his might, breaking her nose. He then punches the living daylights out of her. She falls to the ground, dropping her knife.

Darren turns to Judy. "Thank God, love, you're alright." He takes out his gun and shoots Ginger in the head without even looking. His aim was perfect.

Judy flinches at the sight of this. Her head starts spinning out of control. This was all too much, too soon. She's on the verge of collapsing, and Darren sees this.

He rushes to her and holds her safely in his arms. "I think it's time I tell you the whole truth."

She looks back at him, all bug-eyed. She was still processing everything that had happened. There were 4 dead bodies and millions of pounds of cash in her flat. She was never getting her deposit back.

—X—

CHAPTER 26

A WHOLE TRUTH LATER

Darren drives Dave's car with a shell-shocked Judy. She had just finished hearing the whole truth from him. Every bit of it. Darren didn't leave out any detail. Not even Bob's severed hand. She had been given a lot to process in a short amount of time and it overloaded her brain. She didn't know how to react to any of it. So she just peered out the window, trying to keep her mind occupied with less gruesome thoughts. She had barely spoken since they left her flat in a mad dash. They had just grabbed the bags of money and left everything else behind. Including their lives.

Darren kept thinking about how all his friends had been killed. It was only a few days ago they were all laughing and drinking together. And now they were just gone. They were lifeless corpses. Food for maggots. He would never get to see them again. Never have a drink and smoke with them again. All those memories they shared together would remain just that. Memories. The only solace he could find was that the people who had killed them were in turn killed by him. And Judy.

He turns his gaze to her. She was looking out at the view. She looked broken. Very unlike how she usually was. He wishes she didn't have to go through any of this. He did his best to keep these two worlds of his apart. But they did finally come crashing into each other in the worst way imaginable. And this would change her forever. He recalled the first time he killed someone. How that moment stayed with him and haunted him for days on end. How he couldn't sleep for weeks afterwards. The images kept flashing in front of him over and over again until he felt like he was going insane. And now Judy would go through all of this too. He had to be there for her. He had to help her through this. He had to make sure that when it's all said and done, she could go back to feeling like herself. If that was even possible anymore. Did he ever go back to how he was after his first kill? Or did he become someone else?

But Darren, at his core, was a positive person. At least he thought he was. So he tried his best to find a silver lining in all of this. One of them was that they now had 4 million pounds instead of 2. But he would much rather have all his friends back. Even over his 2 million. But the money would help Judy, his mum, and him disappear in the countryside forever. That kind of money can buy a lot of silence. But would they truly be safe with the trail of blood and violence that was left behind? Louie James would not stop till he found him. And knowing it was him would only enrage Louie further. And then of course, there was the fuzz. These murders were going to create a media storm, and the coppers would have to be extra vigilant and thorough to get to the bottom of these crimes. And they would find all the evidence they would need at the crime scenes. Darren couldn't find a silver lining in any of this. All he knew was that he was ready to do anything to keep Judy and his mum safe. He had Judy with her, and now they were heading to his mum's home in Harrow. He turns once more to look at Judy and wonders what she was thinking about at that moment?

Judy kept having flashes of the corpses back at her flat. The blood oozing out of them. They were living, breathing, functioning humans until they weren't. And she was responsible for killing 2 of them. They were not good men. They had threatened her. They would have killed her if she hadn't killed them. But none of that changed the fact that she took their lives. She had blood on her hands, and nothing was going to wash it away.

She touches her hands to make sure they're still hers. They were trembling with unease. She did her best to clasp them tightly so they wouldn't move. But it didn't help. They felt like a burden that was weighing her down and pulling her into a quicksand of unpleasant thoughts. There was something more on her hands that she felt.

A beautiful gold ring with intricate etchings and a diamond as a centrepiece. She glances at Darren who was doing his best to concentrate on the road. She did love him, but things weren't that simple anymore. Him being in prison was one thing. That was in the past. But what he had gotten himself into now was a whole other mess. And it got messier every step of the way. And she had been unwillingly dragged into it. Even the ring she wore was bought with stolen money. It was evidence of a crime that had been committed.

She knew Darren loved her and would do anything to protect her and his mum. But would he be able to protect himself? The people he stole from killed all his friends. Sooner or later, they would come for him. And Patricia and her if they were in the way. And this is the man she was planning to spend the rest of her life with. But how much longer would his life be? There was already too much on her mind. She was feeling nauseous again. She threw up in the morning, and this long drive made her feel like she needed to hurl again. And her cycle was off. She was late. That was the cherry on top of the shit cake her life had become. She just had to stay strong and hope for the best. And think things through.

Darren parks the car in a quiet North West London suburb. "Babe, we've reached my mum's."

She looks at Darren and nods.

She rushes inside to the facilities as soon as she enters Patricia's. She threw up for twenty minutes before she was sure there was nothing else left to get rid of. She felt hollow and empty afterwards.

Outside Darren told his mum the truth as he had told her. Judy hoped Patricia took it a lot better than she did. But none of it was going to be easy.

She washes her face rigorously, hoping it would wash her tears away. It didn't work. She then downed half a bottle of mouthwash, trying to get rid of the taste of vomit from her mouth. This, at least, did work. Now her breath smelt of vomit and Listerine. It was still an improvement.

But all these were distractions. She kept eyeing something on the counter. Placed right next to a bottle of cheap perfume. It had been 2 minutes. The result would have come in by now. She would know with a simple glance the reason for her morning sickness and why she was late. She takes a deep breath and picks up the pregnancy test. It was as she feared. The crazy thing was that a few hours ago when she bought the test, she had hoped for this result. Now… Now things were different. But at least now she knew what had to be done. She takes a deep breath.

She steps outside to see Patricia sunk in an armchair. The news had hit her just as she expected. She gestures for Darren to come to her.

He comes to her with remorse in his eyes.

"How is your mum holding up?"

"This is the most devastated I've ever seen her. Even more than when Dad…" Darren stops. "And it's all my fault."

She holds his hands. "I'm going to make this as brief and blunt as possible. I love you. I still do.

A part of me still wants to spend the rest of my life with you."

He smiles.

"But! For any of this to become a reality, you have to do some things for me."

"I'll do anything you ask," he reassures her.

"I want you to take all the money and give it back to Louie. Work things out with him. Apologise for everything. Make sure he leaves us alone. I need you to do that."

Darren agrees. "I will."

"And... We leave for the States tonight. I'm buying tickets. We'll go to my parents' home in Providence. And then figure out what to do. But one thing is for sure. We're never coming back here ever again. I will wait for you at Heathrow. If you don't reach on time, then this is the last you'll ever see of me. Can you do all this for me?"

Darren clasps her hands tightly. "Yes. I will. This money means nothing to me if I don't have you in my life. I will sort everything out with Louie. I promise."

Judy half-smiles and nods. This was the only way she saw them having a life together. She kept trying to imagine a life with Darren and their child in America. It could work out; she kept trying to convince herself. She needed it to be a reality. She loved him that much. And now it was his turn to prove how much he loved her.

—— CHAPTER 27 ——

MONEY, WAR, AND PEACE

Louie ponders over different designs while sketching one out. He was detailing a short cocktail dress that would turn men's heads. But he knew that he would wear it with a certain grace and panache no woman could ever pull off. It was his creation, and he made it first for himself, then the world. This was true for all his designs. And he only wore what he designed himself.

He did his best to keep himself occupied with his legal profession while he waited for Ginger along with Dumb & Dumber to get back to him. They had been gone for several hours now. But he hadn't heard back. He wasn't worried but he was curious about what happened. He needed answers. He needed them now.

There's a sharp knock on his cabin door. "But how could that be?" He had the front door locked, and if anyone wanted entry, they would have to ring the bell or break open the lock.

He opens his drawer and takes out a gun. Takes aim at the door. "Come in," he bellows. The door swings open and Louie can't believe his eyes. He thinks he's seeing the ghost of Christmas past. "No! It can't be. What are you doing here?"

It was Darren. He had cleaned himself up before leaving his mum's. He gives a cheeky smile to Louie. "I'm just here to make things right." He picks up the bags of money he had kept aside and tosses them inside the cabin. Opens one of them to show Louie its contents. "Just here to return what belongs to you."

Louie is confused. He places his gun on the table in front of him. He gestures Darren to take a seat, which he does. "How? What's happening? Where are my people?"

Darren makes himself comfortable in the chair. "Let me answer all of those questions. My mates and I stole the money. I'm here to bring it back. I killed your people after they killed mine."

Louie picks up his gun again and points it at him. "And you think you can waltz in here, give it back and pretend like nothing ever happened? The love of my life has been killed. And my assistant, who was my closest confidant. There will be retaliation."

Darren smiles. "Let's not get too excited. I don't want to pull off a Han Solo here." He had his gun pointed at Louie since the moment he sat down.

Louie understands the predicament he's in and puts his gun back down on the table.

"Thank you. I'm glad we can have a discussion like civilised men. Which I know we are," Darren places his gun on his lap.

"What do you want?"

"Peace."

Louie laughs. "You kill the ones closest to me, steal a large part of my money and now you want peace?"

"We only killed the three lovely people who visited us today. And Matt."

Hearing Matt's name came as a shock to Louie. "Then who killed my lover and assistant?"

"I wish I knew. I broke into your office Friday night to empty the vault and steal the key. Your assistant was already dead, shot right in the chest. And the love of your life was found by Bob exactly as you found him. Well except for the neighbour."

"How do I know you're telling the truth?"

"Why would I lie? If I wanted to, I could have just disappeared with the money. I promise you and the Bobbys would not have been able to find me."

"Oh, we would have. And you expect me to believe that the two people closest to me were just dead while you stole my money."

"I don't care if you believe me or not. It's the truth."

Louie thinks about what Darren had said. He takes a good, long look at him. Darren is calm and collected. "Let's assume you're telling the truth."

"I am."

"I'm still confused about certain details. How did you know where all my money was hidden?"

Darren smiles. "Now you're asking the right questions. Such details can only be known by someone close to you. So tell me, who is that close to you? Who would know all these things? I'm sure it can't be more than a handful of people."

"Answer me first. How did you get to know all these things?"

"From the person who hired us. He had all the details penned down. All we had to do was what was told of us. And we did."

"Who hired you?"

Darren giggles. "Now this is where things get tricky. We don't know his name."

Louie slams his table. "What insolence is this? You did a job for someone without knowing who they were?"

"Yes."

"Why?"

"Because he offered me 2 million pounds for a few hours of work."

Louie thinks about Darren's answer. He hated to admit it, but he believed him. "So what do you know about him?"

"He goes by Mr. Shadow."

"Shadow?"

"No! Mr Shadow. He was very clear on that."

Louie is confused but accepts what's being told to him. "Okay! Anything else you know about him?"

"He called us in the middle of the night. Met us and gave us the details. And then we did the job."

"If you've met him, then you would know what he looks like?"

"It's more complicated than that. We couldn't get a good look at him. At all. All we know for sure is that he's tall, lean, and white."

"How is it more complicated than that?"

"Can you tell what a woman looks like if she's wearing a burqa?"

"But he wasn't wearing a fucking burqa!"

"Can we just agree to disagree? The point is that this Mr Shadow, whoever he is, is someone who was close to you. That's why he knew such intimate details about you, like where you had hidden your money."

"You were also close to me once. In my inner circle," Louie retorts.

"Yeah, but not close enough to know where you hid your money," Darren smiles to hide his pain. "Or close enough not to be sold out to the fuzz."

Louie looks Darren in the eye. "Still bitter about that, huh?"

"No, why should I? I mean, I only lost 2 years of my life and any future prospects to get a good job."

"Yeah, that would make someone mad enough to plot the perfect revenge. Like killing their closest people and stealing 5 million pounds from them."

"I agree. But I didn't do the planning. I did, however, enjoy stealing from you. It felt like karmic justice. You got what you deserved."

"Cry me a fucking river. You can't imagine the pain I'm in. Everything I ever cherished has been snatched from me. And I couldn't do anything about it."

Darren laughs. "Oh, you think I don't? My three closest mates have been killed right in front of me. And there's nothing I could do about it either."

Louie understands Darren's perspective. They both carried the same pain. "Then what do you suggest?"

"I just want peace. I don't want the money. I don't want any more bloodshed. The person who planned this… This Mr Shadow is someone who knew intimate personal details about you. Find him and you'll find the person who killed your closest people," Darren gets up to leave. "I wish you the best of luck. And I'm sorry we stole your money."

Louie ponders over everything Darren had said. He had a lot of questions answered, but there were more questions that popped up in his head.

"Wait! Please," Louie asks instead of commanding. That was new for him. "Why did you choose peace? You could have made a run for it?"

Darren almost has tears in his eyes. "Because all the money in the world isn't as important to me as the love of my life. And if we can have peace for us, then I'm already the richest man in the world. And happiest too."

Louie smiles. "Never thought I'd see Darren Turner choose a woman over money. You have changed."

"You haven't," Darren snaps back. "Maybe you should, Louie."

This truly hits Louie. Maybe Darren was right. Maybe he did need to change. And he needed to rethink how he went about his life. But all of that had to wait. He had got his money back, but what he truly wanted was vengeance and reparations. And he needed some muscle for it. And he was willing to pay top dollar for it.

Darren is at the door when Louie calls out to him again. "One more thing before you leave."

Darren turns around.

"Where did you have your meeting with Mr. Shadow?"

"Yes, I suppose I do have one more thing to share with you. Give me a pen, and I'll write it down."

Louie smiles. "I have a better proposition."

"I'm all ears."

"Take me there. And then leave in peace."

Darren isn't convinced.

"With 2 million."

Darren was now convinced. It was as easy as that. He smiles. "We'll take your car or mine?"

CHAPTER 28

THE END

Darren sat shotgun while Louie drove them to Mr Shadow's lair in his Benz with the fishnet bumper sticker. They carried the 2 million in cash with them. Louie was more than willing to keep his end of the bargain if Darren didn't try and fuck him over. And it was good to have someone as foolhardy as Darren on his side when confronting someone as enigmatic and dangerous as Mr Shadow. This man knew too much about him. He was tall, lean and white. That was all that was known. But who could it be? In Louie's mind, it had to be a former lover or a discarded confidant. But there were a few of them who matched that description. Hell, even Darren matched that description. But it couldn't be him planning everything. Could it? Louie just wasn't sure anymore. Everyone's reality and perception of life were thrown off-kilter when Mr Shadow got involved with them. He glances at Darren briefly and wonders what he's thinking about. He was awfully quiet for someone who never knew when to shut the fuck up. But Louie supposed that prison probably changed him. He was willing to give up 4 million pounds just to be with the love of his life. But Louie was willing to give up even more to find out who killed his. The 2 million he was giving to Darren to help him was peanuts.

The silence of the drive started getting to Louie, who was easily bored. They were still a bit away from their destination, so he decided to fill it with some conversation. "You remember that job in Canary Wharf? That was a fun time, wasn't it."

"Not interested in any reminiscing. Thank you. We don't need to bond." Darren did remember that job. It was a cherished memory. He had that safe open in no time. They were in and out of that place in a snap. The same reason Louie bought it up. He knew how to make anyone feel special if he wanted to. Darren was in no mood for that.

Louie knew a dead end when he saw one. He turned on the stereo and tuned it to a station playing the classics. Not the distraction he had in mind, but it would do.

Darren sat quietly. For a change, he wasn't anxious either. He had no idea what awaited Louie and him at Mr Shadow's lair, but he was ready for anything. Because he knew that at the end of it, he would get to be with Judy. Nothing else mattered to him anymore. He texted her before they left for Mr Shadow's, informing her of everything. He told Louie he wouldn't come unless he kept her in the loop. He showed Louie the text while sending it to prove he was not going to double-cross him. Louie believed him. And he should because, for once in his life, Darren wasn't lying about anything. Judy was worried that Darren was risking his life again for the promise of 2 million, but the 2 million was a strong enough motivator for her to agree. That money would help them build a luxurious life together in the States. So she told him the same thing she said at Patricia's. She's going to be waiting for him. First at his mum's, then at Heathrow. If he can make it in time, then they'll be together. And he intended to be there on time.

The sun was setting by the time they parked next to Flaming Nero's. Darren takes one last good look at it. He hated working there, but he was grateful he had something to pay the bills after prison. He puts on his hat.

"How much further is it from here?" Louie asks impatiently. He couldn't wait to learn more about

Mr. Shadow and was hoping he was lucky enough to find him there in the flesh.

"Just a few alleys down. I'm carrying the bag of money with me. I'll show you where this cunt met us, and then I'm off. A deal's a deal," Darren wanted to make sure Louie understood.

"Deal's a deal," Louie agrees.

Darren is about to lead Louie to Mr Shadow's lair but stops. Something else was gnawing at him. "One more thing before we do this."

"What is it now?"

"Why didn't you bail me out?"

Louie is about to answer.

Darren interjects before he can. "The truth. Nothing else. Don't sugarcoat it."

Louie nods. "Matt found someone better."

Darren can't believe it. "That's it?"

"Yeah! It's just business. Nothing personal."

Darren is taken aback. He didn't know what to expect. But he was hurt for sure. "I can't believe there was a time when I was in awe of you."

Louie couldn't care less about Darren's feelings. "I'm still in awe of me."

And Darren understood. Like Louie said. It was just business. And that's what Darren was here to do. Nothing more. Nothing less. He nods in acceptance and leads the way.

They make their short walk to Mr Shadow's lair. Before long, they reach the fabled door in the alley. It was locked.

"I'm guessing opening this is a piece of piss for you," Louie jests.

Darren was in no mood to jest. He just wanted to get done with this. He takes out a small box of tools from his trench coat pocket and within moments undoes the lock.

The door swings open noiselessly as the remaining remnants of daylight enters the dark void of Mr Shadow's lair. Darren and Louie look at each other and nod. They take out their guns and enter. They close the door behind them.

Darren uses his phone as a flashlight as they walk down the narrow corridor and enter the room where Mr Shadow had met them. Darren recalled the light being shone on his face while

Mr Shadow sat in front of him in silhouette. Like a shadow.

Darren looks briefly for the light switch and finds it. He flicks it on and reveals an empty, barren room. The only thing left behind was the light that Mr Shadow blasted on their faces and an envelope on the floor in a corner, which Darren didn't see, but Louie did.

Darren is confused. The last time he was here, there were cabinets filled with files, a table in the centre, and chairs on either side. He couldn't believe it. He goes to the light. The only thing that was still there from the last time he was here.

"No, it can't be. Where is everything? It was all here just yesterday. All those files of research and planning that Mr Shadow had done. I swear."

Darren's rant didn't help Louie empathise with him. His attention and gaze were at the envelope. Nothing else. He goes to it and picks it up. He turns it around and sees that it was addressed to him. In bold letters. He opens it while...

... Darren continues his derelict rant. "This was the light that he had on behind him. It kept him silhouetted. All we could see was a shadow." Darren tries to turn the light on.

Louie opens the envelope and takes out the letter inside. He begins to read.

Louie,

If you're reading this, then I have won. I've brought you exactly where I wanted to. This is, after all, the final step in my master plan. You deserve every bit of what is coming to you.

Yours truly,
Mr. Shadow

Louie finishes reading the letter. His hands begin to tremble, and goosebumps dot his arms and legs. "I've walked into a trap," he thinks to himself.

At that moment, Darren is finally able to get the light to turn on. It nearly blinds him, and he turns around to face Louie.

Louie looks back at Darren, but he can't see him. He can only see a silhouette: a tall, lean man wearing a trench coat and a hat. He looked exactly like how Darren described Mr Shadow, except it was Darren. But maybe, just maybe, it was Mr Shadow.

Louie crumples the letter in his hands as seething rage takes over. He takes out his gun and points it at Darren. "So this is why you brought me here. To finish your master plan."

Darren is confused but sees a gun pointed at him. "What are you going on about?"

Louie laughs. "It's okay. You don't have to lie anymore. I've read your little note. I know the truth, Darren. Or should I say… Mr Shadow."

Darren has no idea what Louie is talking about. All that mattered was that he had a gun pointed at him. "Have you gone stark raving mad? I am not Mr Shadow. Why does everyone keep thinking that? Now put that gun down before someone gets hurt."

"Oh, someone is going to get hurt."

Louie takes aim and shoots. He barely misses Darren. With the light shining directly on him, it was hard to aim. He shoots again repeatedly but misses. One of the bullets hits the light, shattering the bulb into a million little pieces.

Darren had had enough. He tackles Louie with all his might and knocks him down. The gun drops from Louie's hand. Darren punches Louie repeatedly in the face, but it does little to stop him. Louie overpowers Darren easily and tosses him aside like a ragdoll.

Louie gets back on his feet and kicks Darren around like a helpless stray dog. "This is for Anthony." He kicks Darren in the face.

Darren rolls over in pain. Louie then stomps him on his ribs, cracking a few in the process. Darren was now finding it hard to breathe. He just lay there writhing in pain. He was probably bleeding internally. Darren just looked at Louie helplessly. His eyes were filled with a fear he never experienced before.

Louie takes off his heels, which are still caked with dry blood. He holds Darren down, choking him with his left hand. With his right, he takes aim at Darren's skull. He was going to cave it in with his heel like he had done countless times before.

Darren watched the heel tip go up and knew he had mere moments to act. Or this would be his end. But he wanted to fight. He had to. He needed to. His love for Judy told him not to give up. Not yet! With his arms under Louie's weight, he had only one course of action. He kicks

Louie in the crotch hard with his knee, making him squeal like a pig. Louie's loosens his grip around Darren's neck. Darren sees this opening and bites Louie on his left hand like a rabid dog escaping the pound. Louie tends to his bleeding hand, giving Darren enough wiggle room to free himself and stand firmly back on his two feet.

Darren's head was spinning, and his vision was blurry. All he could see was the lightbulb dangling from the ceiling. It looked like a halo. He takes out his gun.

Louie looks at the bite marks on his left hand and simmers in rage. He eyes his gun on the floor next to him and picks it up with his right hand. He pushes himself on his feet, takes aim at Darren and shoots.

BANG! A bullet hits Louie square on his right hand. He drops his gun. Both his hands were now of no use. He looks up and sees Darren taking aim at him.

Darren shoots Louie right in the chest. Two shots. Clean and precise. Professional hits with very little blood splatter. Louie falls to the ground, bleeding and gasping for air.

Darren puts on his hat and stands over him. The only light in the room now was the small bare light bulb that hung overhead. Louie takes one last look at Darren's face. Except he could barely make out anything except his eyes. The dangling light was behind Darren's head and all Louie saw was the same silhouette as before. He was still convinced Darren was Mr Shadow. But the truth didn't matter anymore. All that mattered was the predicament he was in. And he makes peace with it. He accepts his fate. He had lost and Mr Shadow had won. Mr Shadow had had his revenge. He looks Darren in the eyes and nods.

Darren nods back. He takes aim at Louie's face and shoots him. That was the end of Louie James, high street fashion designer extraordinaire by day, drug lord by night. Darren takes a deep breath of relief.

He drops the gun right then and there. He takes out the car keys from Louie's handbag. He picks up his bag of money and rushes out without a moment to waste.

A few minutes later he's driving Louie's Benz with the 2 million. He texted Judy he's on his way. He had won. He couldn't believe it. With Louie dead, only the coppers was after him now. And maybe Mr Shadow. All he needed to do to be safe was to leave London for the States tonight. And then he and Judy could have the life they dreamed of. He would need to leave instructions with his mum on how to send the money over to them, but that could all be managed without much work.

It took him forty minutes to reach his mum's. He runs inside with the bag of money. Judy was there waiting for him. She smiles as soon as she sees him. He tosses the bag aside and takes her in his arms. They kiss passionately.

"I love you, Judy."

"I love you too."

"I promised I'd get back to you safely."

"And you kept that promise."

"Anything and everything for you."

Judy hugs him tightly. He feels some pain in his gut. He lets out a scream. She lets go of him. "Are you alright?"

"I am. Just a bit of pain in the gut," Darren takes a look at the source of the pain. His coat was drenched. He opens it. He was bleeding. He was shot in the gut. He briefly remembers Louie shooting at him right before he shot him in the hand. He hadn't noticed.

Judy looks at him with tears in her eyes. "Are you alright?"

Darren tries to respond, but he can't. The words don't come out of his mouth.

She asks again, this time loudly. "Are you alright?"

He tries to answer but can't.

"Are you alright?" she says again, but this time she sounds like a man.

Darren wakes up. He's still in Louie's car with the bag of money next to him. He had crashed the car into a streetlight which was shining like a halo. The airbag had been deployed. He was bleeding profusely because of the gunshot.

Standing next to him was a man. "Mate, can you hear me? Are you alright?"

Darren looks at him with the last bit of life in him and smiles. His vision becomes blurry, and all he can see is blinding light. He imagines it to be heaven. All he does is smile. "I'm coming to you, God," he blurts out as his soul begins leaving his body.

The man is confused about what Darren is saying.

Darren smiles as he imagines himself walking up a stairway to heaven. He sees the source of the blinding light. It was something he couldn't explain. It was everything but nothing. It was blinding yet comforting. It was God in all its opulence. Darren was at peace and had accepted his fate. What else could he do? He walks to God and is comforted by the divine presence. It was serene all around him. With God, he knew he would have answers to the questions that had bothered him during his mortal life. He wanted to ask a lot of questions, but one stood out above all. It felt rather pressing to know. And it left him conflicted.

God speaks to him in a comforting, soulful voice. "What is bothering you, my son? Ask away."

Darren felt comforted by God's words. The illuminating light seemed to heal all that could ail him. He smiled and asked the one question that he needed an answer for.

"God, who is Mr Shadow?"

—X—

www.ingramcontent.com/pod-product-compliance
Lightning Source LLC
Chambersburg PA
CBHW021424150726
47989CB00001B/104